the insiders
j. minter

BLOOMSBURY

First published in Great Britain in 2004 by Bloomsbury Publishing Plc,
38 Soho Square, London, W1D 3HB

Produced by 17th Street Productions, an Alloy company
151 West 26th Street
New York, NY 10001

ISBN 0 7475 7114 7

All papers used by Bloomsbury Publishing are natural, recyclable products
made from wood grown in well managed forests. The manufacturing
processes conform to the environmental regulations
of the country of origin.

Printed in Great Britain by Clays Ltd, St Ives plc

10 9 8 7 6 5 4 3 2 1

for **MBB**

a few words from me, jonathan, the social glue

We met Patch in fifth grade and let him into our gang right away. Before that we were four— Arno Wildenburger, Mickey Pardo, David Grobart, and me. My name is Jonathan.

Back then we had to dress for school in blue polo shirts and khakis, so we looked weirdly alike. And our parents were either friends or were doing business with each other. Those things, plus the fact that we'd all been in school together since kindergarten, were more than reason enough for us to be best friends. We picked each other for dodgeball, shared our science home-work, and said laser when we meant penis.

Then Patch showed up. He was a skater whose family had lived on a sailboat since he was six. That experience left him with heavy freckles, streaky blond hair, and a weird kind of laid-back quality, where even though we had bells between classes, he'd get up and sit down when he felt like it, because even indoors he was telling time by the sun.

We were eleven, and Patch was the *man*. The girls were all obsessed with him. Why? He barely noticed them, that's why. He didn't play too rough with them like Mickey or tease them like Arno. And he didn't sulk when they didn't talk to him like David. Since we were the cool group, we grabbed him, because we were as confused and amazed by him as anyone. And that made us five.

Patch was so cool that sometimes he forgot to wear shoes to school. He had heavy-lidded eyes and he'd stand and mutter apologies at teachers until they would give him anything. As for the rest of us: Arno was better looking than everybody else, and sharper. His polo shirts came from some special store on Madison Avenue and his black hair stayed in place even when we were beating on each other. He always had this level glare and he wasn't afraid to use it. Mickey was crazy back then, too. He'd talk back to anybody, anytime. David was always good at sports and considered the normal one, though he was kind of neurotic, if I can use that word about a fifth grader.

We were all fooling around with girls. We

thought it was funny to call it "Seven Minutes in Heaven." Now we're sixteen and we don't call it anything in particular, but we sure do a lot of it.

Then, at the end of fifth grade, Arno kissed this girl Molly who David liked. And David moped about it and we couldn't stop them from doing some serious fighting at a sleepover at Patch's country house in Greenwich. After that we made a pact about not kissing girls that one of us had clearly said we liked, even if the girls asked. It was Patch who begged us not to bother making any other rules. He knew he'd never remember to follow them. So that was our only promise to each other.

I was always trying to get us to stick together. They called me "the glue." This was before my parents got divorced and my dad went to live in London, so I don't have a clue why I was like that, like some shepherd, but I was always gathering us up. It was like I felt better when I could have us all in the room. I thought if we were together, we were better than safe. We were the Insiders. But we never, never called ourselves that.

There were the five of us, and up to about the time this story starts, that seemed like enough.

friday night makes a fine beginning . . .

get ready to deal with my cousin . . . kelli

"Thanks for letting me come out with you," Kelli said. There was a bit of midwestern twang in her voice that was both sweet and a little grating.

"We'll definitely have fun," I said, and left it at that because of course her coming out with me wasn't my idea. It was my mom's. We were in the backseat of my mom's town car, which we'd been told to *send right back* to Nobu, after we got dropped off at Patch's house on Perry Street.

"Do you want to tell me about them?" Kelli asked.

"Who?"

"Whoever we're going to see," Kelli said, and laughed. She didn't seem uncomfortable or anything. If I were her I would've been, because we were on our way to a party in the West Village, with my best friends, and Kelli was my cousin from St. Louis, and there's no way she could've guessed what she was about to see.

Kelli was good-looking, in a bleach-haired, Brittany Murphy sort of way. She'd gotten done up in a short white skirt and pink sweater for the big welcome-to-the-city dinner with her mom and my mom and about a half dozen other people, including my mom's yoga instructor and her business partner.

And then, when our moms were sipping their Amarettos and waiting for the bento boxes of chocolate soufflé and vanilla ice cream they wouldn't eat, I decided to get out of there. I got on my Blackberry to Arno, and looked around for the yellow Ralph corduroy blazer I was into that week. Then my mom said "*bring her with you*" in a stage whisper. Like that was funny.

Kelli said, "Yeah, bring me!" in a very throaty voice. How was I going to say no? My mom doesn't tell me what to do very often, but obviously she wanted to keep drinking and reminiscing with her recently divorced sister and I knew that if I didn't get out of there, with Kelli, I was going to hear about it later.

Kelli had come from St. Louis with her mom to visit NYU and Sarah Lawrence and Barnard. She was a senior in high school, and I was a junior, and in the three years since I'd last seen her, it looked like she'd gotten a little less risk-averse, to put it lightly. Or, she'd been *around*. But then again, *around* had been the St. Louis suburbs, which is fine, I'm sure, but it's not like New York City.

"It's hard to explain," I said. We were at Canal Street. My knee was jerking uncontrollably. I crossed my legs and rubbed at my brown suede JP Tod's loafers.

"What is?" she asked. She had a good voice. Her eyes were green and sort of angled in toward her nose. Cat eyes. She was tall, too. So yes, she was sexy, but in a cheerleader-gone-bad kind of way. And nobody I know has cheerleaders at their school, which is a good way of beginning to explain why I was not that excited about introducing her to everybody.

"About my friends—it's really hard to get us all in one place at one time."

"Is that like, your job?"

"No. Not exactly. It's just—they're really good guys but we go to different schools now and I'm the underlying thing that keeps us together."

"The underlying thing?"

"More like the master of ceremonies," I said. "But of course nothing like that."

"Whatever," she said. "I'm just psyched to get

away from my mom." She pulled out a mirror and began painting on some pink lipstick. Worst case was I'd have to put her in a cab and send her back to my house, where her mom had one of the guest bedrooms and she had my brother Ted's room, since he was now a freshman up at Vassar. No. Worst case was Kelli would get wrecked and end up sleeping on the floor in Patch's kitchen with her arms curled around a chair leg and a quart bottle of crème de menthe. My aunt Jane would bitch me out to no end. I watched Kelli stare out the window as we got deep into the West Village. She seemed really excited by it all—it was like her whole body was hungry for Manhattan.

"I came to the city at the beginning of last year," she said. "It was right after my mom kicked my dad out so my parents weren't keeping very good track of things and me and a bunch of other girls drove here and we had a total blast. We barely had time to get out of the car—but just driving around for two hours in Times Square, that was wild."

"Yeah," I sniffed. "Wild."

Andy, my mom's driver, pulled over on Greenwich and Perry.

"Thanks, man," I said. As usual, Andy said nothing.

It was early October and cool out. It had rained earlier and fat drops fell on our heads from the trees on Perry. Maybe the street glistened a little. I was trying to not be so analytic and nervous, to just give in to the fact that the night was beautiful and full of promises, even with Kelli along. I straightened my jacket, flipped out the collar on my white Prada button-down, and shrugged the hair out of my eyes.

"You didn't explain anything," Kelli said as I helped her out of the car. "What about a girl-friend? Do you have one? Are we going to meet her?"

"No," I said. I didn't want to mention Liza. Or that other thing I was involved with, which I didn't even want to go into.

"Don't worry," I said. "You'll meet everybody. Arno's the hot guy who looks like you've seen him in magazines 'cause you probably have, Mickey's basically crazy, and David's completely introverted and overly sensitive. Patch is never around—but this is his house. That's all you need to know."

And then we were up close to Patch's house and I could already hear a bootleg Neptunes track rattling the Floods' town house windows.

We ran up the steps to Patch's door and hit the

buzzer. The door was big, white, and vibrating. So were the windows. Everything else was bright red brick. The music switched to the new Yeah Yeah Yeah's and I checked my shoes once more as the door opened. I also heard the noise of a window above us going up so I knew that somebody was looking down, but I didn't look, 'cause that would have gotten me into this whole other thing with Flan Flood, Patch's little sister, and it absolutely was not the right time for that.

"Oh wow," Kelli said. I didn't look behind me. I knew she'd be staring with those hungry eyes and I didn't want to see that again.

"Well, if it isn't Jonathan. And who is this?" Arno asked.

"This is my cousin Kelli," I said. "Arno, close your mouth—she's from St. Louis."

"Your mom's sister's little girl," Arno said.

"You've heard about me?" Kelli asked.

"Nah—wild guess," Arno said. He started laughing as he pulled us both into the house. Arno's half Brazilian and half German. His mom and dad are art dealers and he lives in a town house in Chelsea that's filled with huge art. He really does model, too, for magazines like *Black Book*. He's six foot one and better looking than anyone I've ever met. He was wearing a ripped purple polo shirt, Helmut Lang jeans, and Gucci loafers.

"Where you been?" he asked, and burped.

"Family dinner."

"I hope you at least got to slam down some good wine," he said.

We'd put all the expensive stuff in Patch's living room away earlier that day. Then we lit several dozen candles and put them in all the nooks where the sculptures and stuff had been. We'd pulled all the couches into a loose circle and thrown every pillow we could find on the floor, so the living room looked like one of those new super-sleek hotel bars in downtown L.A. Then we'd hauled a dozen cases of beer down to the ground-floor kitchen. Already at least twenty kids were drifting up and down the stairs, getting beer, and forming groups for drinking games.

"Wow," Kelli said. She was staring at Arno, like she'd saved up all her allowance and now she wanted to buy him.

"Where's Patch?" I asked Arno.

"Stop it," Arno said. "I don't know." Some girl from Spence came up and started swinging on Arno's arm.

As usual, Patch Flood, who was our whole reason to be there, was nowhere to be seen. He's the kind of guy who wears the same khakis for six months until they harden up and have to be removed with gardening scissors because he's so forgetful and messy and just . . . just so *cool* about it. He's like a guy who floats by you on a happy cloud. You jump up and try to get him, but he's always out of reach.

Patch's parents are at their estate in Greenwich most of the time, so they've practically deeded the Perry Street house to their kids: Patch, Zed, who is up at Vassar with my brother, and Patch's big sister February, who is twenty and currently taking her second year off before college while supposedly doing an internship at Alvin Adler's design studio in Tribeca. Then there's little Flannery, known as Flan, a cute eighth grader who may or may not have been at the window when I came in with Kelli.

Arno pulled me into the dining room, stepping in some freshman girl's lap while he moved—and she seemed to cradle his foot for a second before he pulled away.

"Where'd you say you picked this *Kelli* up?" Arno asked. "The West Side Highway for twenty bucks and a Happy Meal?"

"I said she was my cousin," I said.

"Class runs thinner than water in your family," Arno said.

"At least my parents aren't art dealers," I said. It wasn't that I thought Arno's parents weren't cool. But Arno's easy to confuse—we have English class together at Gissing Academy and I'm always feeding him nonsense to say. Then he says whatever I come up with so charmingly to our teacher, Ms. Rodale, that she convinces herself that the junk I told him to say makes sense. It's a vicious circle and now my whole class agrees that P. Diddy is basing his whole existence on the world Fitzgerald built in *The Great Gatsby*.

"Mickey was looking for you. He broke into Philippa's house earlier and her dad called the cops," Arno said.

"Was he upset?" I asked.

"Jackson Frady? No, he loves it when Mickey does that," Arno said. "He asked him to set their house on fire next time."

"Don't crack wise," I said. "You can't keep it up."

Arno didn't answer. Instead, he threw an arm over my shoulder and we started punching each other's ribs.

"Where's the beer?" Kelli shouted over the music. She definitely wanted a do-over with Arno. He smiled at her, let go of me, and took her by the hand.

"You want to show her where she can get her drink on?" I asked.

"Would you put it that way?" Arno said to Kelli. But her grin for him was so big that she couldn't answer, and when Arno saw it, he started laughing, too. I eyed the staircase. Flan was up there. Probably in bed. She always got up early to ride horses in Central Park on Saturdays.

Somebody grabbed my lapel and I grabbed his arm and tried to rip his hand off my clothes.

It was David. "Have you seen Amanda?" he asked. He had his Yale sweatshirt on and the hood was pulled over his head. I tugged it off. He pulled it back on. He was the tallest of all of us. David was the best basketball player at Potterton. He was a really good listener, and, save for some deep neuroses, an all-around normal guy. So somehow, between good listening and being one of us five, he'd gotten this hot girl, Amanda Harrison Deutschmann, who was absolutely the most conniving person I'd ever met. Partly because of her, he was David the Mope.

"I haven't seen her tonight," I said.

"You sure?"

"Yes, I'm sure. What would I do, lie to you?"

"I hope not," he said. "Would you?"

"David. Why would I? She's your girlfriend. She's probably just not here yet."

"She is. And I can't find her."

"Don't be a mope."

"I can't help it," David said. He walked off, trailing the laces on the vintage '86 Jordans I had bought in Williamsburg from a guy called Shigeto for four hundred dollars. They were way too big for me, so I gave them to David, who had no idea how valuable they were and kept treating them like normal sneakers. I wished he would tie the laces.

More girls came in the door. I didn't recognize them, but I heard them whispering about Patch. Would they even get a chance to see him? If I knew Patch at all, the answer was no. I looked both ways before dashing up the staircase to check in on little Flan Flood.

arno knows exactly where amanda is

Amanda Harrison Deutschmann and Arno Wildenburger were out in Patch's backyard. A very light rain, like a mist, was falling.

"What're you looking at?" Amanda asked. She was a short girl with very straight blond hair, gray-green eyes, and a killer body that she'd gotten from a lot of sailing and tennis.

"You, because you're hot," Arno said.

"Oh yeah?" Amanda said.

"Your eyes are like soft gray clouds on a Saturday afternoon."

"Oh yeah?"

She put her arms around Arno's neck and opened her eyes wider, at him. Arno took a pull from his beer and swayed Amanda back and forth.

Arno had come from a small dinner party his parents had thrown for Randall Oddy, a British painter who was having his opening the following night. He'd done several shots of Jaeger with Randall in the kitchen.

Randall was only twenty-three, after all, and he'd made Arno swear to hang with him the next night at his opening. And then Arno sailed right out of that party and landed here, with David's girlfriend, where he really was not supposed to be.

"Well," Amanda said.

"Well what?" Arno asked. He sort of half-glared at Amanda. She licked her lips, so he glared some more.

"I want to talk to you," Amanda said.

"About what?"

"About . . ." Amanda paused. "I'm upset about Meg."

"Who?"

"You know, my friend from Brearley who passed out in a bathtub at the American Hotel at Sag Harbor last weekend. Her mom had to come all the way out from the city to get her and even now nobody knows how Meg got there. Meg can't remember a thing and we've had to have all these meetings where we try to recreate her night."

"Oh yeah, Meg." Arno slipped his arm around Amanda and she gave in to him. With his other hand he sipped from his bottle of Grolsch. He wasn't drunk. Physically, getting rocked took some work—he was almost as big as David, though he wasn't any good at basketball, and hadn't been since they'd been cocaptains of the middle school team at Grace Church.

He took Amanda's hand in his for a second, and she moved it to his mouth. Did she want him to bite it? He did, and she moaned.

"When we were in sixth grade," Arno said, "Mickey got kicked off the basketball team for biting the hand of some kid on the Saint Ann's team, so David had to be the captain even though Coach Bank said he didn't have leadership qualities. We ended up with a losing season."

"Did you have to mention him?" Amanda asked. She'd slipped her hand underneath Arno's shirt and he was trying to keep his goose bumps under control.

"It feels like you lost something inside my shirt and you're desperate to find it."

"Don't make fun of me," Amanda said. "What we're doing is a big deal."

"Sorry," Arno said.

"I just want to talk to you about what's going on with me," Amanda said.

"Okayyy," Arno said. "What is going on?"

"Right now, you are."

"You're beautiful," Arno said. "You know that? You're built like an eighties Playboy playmate—just like the ones my father has his bathroom wallpapered with. When I was a kid I looked at those all the time."

"You looked at those and then what did you do?" Amanda whispered in his ear.

"Exactly," Arno said.

Arno touched Amanda's round shoulder. He looked around and saw that if someone happened to glance through the windows in the parlor, or in the kitchen, or even on the third floor, they could see what was going on in the garden really easily.

"You know what?" Arno said. "I need to go to the bathroom. I need to go use a bathroom upstairs and you need to come with me."

"No."

"Yes."

"No."

"Okay, forget it," Arno said.

"No . . . well, I'll follow you up there."

Upstairs and tucked safely away in the bathroom, Arno and Amanda got to fooling around pretty seriously. And it was as if she'd been hungry to do something really wrong with him for a while already. They leaned against the white subway tile wall and they both eased their shirts up, like exotic snakes, and then they pulled off their pants, like strippers.

They were trying to be really quiet. Because even though the party was loud, they were on the top floor, and they were in the bathroom that had doors leading to both Flan's and Patch's bedrooms.

During a lull, they heard a soft voice.

"That's a cute story," the voice said. It wasn't Flan's. Arno raised an eyebrow at Amanda, who'd been chewing on his neck. He pried her off, and she listened, too.

"And then tomorrow I'll probably watch movies with my friends after we go riding," a different voice said. That was Flan.

"That sounds nice," said the other voice, which clearly belonged to a guy. "If I didn't have to hang out with my cousin I could probably go up to the park and see you ride."

Then the voice stopped.

"*Jonathan*," Amanda whispered to Arno.

"Nah," Arno said. They both put their ears up to the closed door.

"Don't you go out with Liza Komansky?" Flan asked.

"No way—people said we were going out last year, but that was just because we spent a lot of our time together."

"And fooled around constantly and didn't go out with anybody else," Amanda whispered. "And now look, Jonathan's going after little Flan Flood." Arno kissed her neck. She punched him in the chest. Then there was quiet from Flan's room.

"It sounds like they're fooling around, or maybe just *cuddling*," Arno said.

"No way," Amanda said.

Amanda and Arno started giggling then, and covering each other's mouths. Most of their clothes were off and they were awkwardly leaning against the wall.

So they had to twist around and help each other stand when Jonathan opened the door to the bathroom to see what was going on. And they clearly couldn't figure out what to say when Jonathan leaned in the doorway and stared at them, visibly shocked that Arno was in there with Amanda Harrison Deutschmann, *their best friend David's girlfriend.*

"Shit," Arno whispered. "I really wish you hadn't been the one to see this."

"Because I'm your conscience?" Jonathan hissed.

"That's way too nice a way of putting it," Arno whispered back.

"Jonathan?" Flan called out.

Jonathan pointed to Arno and Amanda and put his finger over his mouth to say *shhh*. Then he pointed to the bedroom behind him, and to himself, and did the whole quiet gesture all over again.

"Nobody can say anything about anybody else," Jonathan whispered. "Get it?"

"Shhh," Arno said, and fixed his eyes on the floor.

"Little Flan Flood," Amanda said, and shook her head. "Jonathan, you are crazy."

"She's just a friend," Jonathan said. "I'm not doing anything with her that could be construed as crazy." But he smiled when he said it, and he went a little red.

"Bullshit," Amanda said.

"We didn't fool around," Jonathan said, glaring at Amanda. "And even if we did, which we didn't, I wouldn't be cheating on somebody who happens to *completely love me.*" The lights in the bathroom were on a dimmer, and Jonathan touched the switch and made everything a little brighter.

They were all glaring at each other.

"Why don't we all leave each other alone," Amanda said, "and go back to what we were doing?"

"No," Arno said. "I think Jonathan's right." He'd found his jeans and he sat down on the lip of the tub to put them on.

"Oh, great," Amanda said, stooping over to gather her clothes. "I hate it when you guys stick together. Jonathan, would you get out of here? Can you not see that I'm practically naked?"

david is depressed

"It looks like you're waiting for something," Kelli said.

"Me? No," David said. "You want anything? I wish I could tell you where Jonathan went."

"I don't care. I think he was happy to get rid of me."

"Oh, I'm sure that's not true," David said. He tried a smile. He was sitting with Kelli in the breakfast nook, a big windowed room off the Floods' kitchen. David had a similar room up at his country house in Saddle River, only his parents called it the greenhouse and had spider plants in all the spots where a person might want to sit.

They were drinking Heineken from little keg-shaped cans and picking at a bowl of dried Chinese peas. David could never figure out the arrangement that the Floods had with their kids—did they know that there were blowouts every weekend? David's parents would barely let his friends in the door. And considering that they were both therapists he found that pretty uncivilized, though he'd never exactly felt free enough to say so. They treated him like he was their age and wouldn't want a bunch of hell-raisers around all their old psychology books and stuff either. He somehow managed to talk to them constantly without ever saying anything meaningful to either of them. He was an only child.

"Do you have a girlfriend?" Kelli asked.

David looked up. His can was full. He realized he was barely drinking at all. Amanda. Where was she?

"Yes."

"Then where is she?"

"I don't know," David mumbled. He could hardly get the words out.

"I wish I could talk to that guy Arno again," Kelli said. "He left me in the middle of a sentence. He seems like a pretty nice guy." She kept clacking her fingernails against the cream-colored table. She was chewing Savage Sour Apple Bubblicious and she gave David a piece.

"Nice?" David asked. "You think Arno is nice?"

"Sure. Don't you think he's nice?"

"No." But David couldn't figure out how to pinpoint why, exactly, he didn't think Arno was nice. Of the five friends, Arno and David were the furthest apart, partly because they'd been the closest back in lower school. Now David trusted Arno the least of any of them. But whenever they were alone, Arno always redeemed himself. He'd been the one who taught David not to walk away when girls said to, and how to lightly brush hair off a girl's forehead and not turn purple at the same time. But lately David had been so obsessed with Amanda that he'd forgotten all those lessons.

"What about you?" Kelli asked. David glanced at her. Now she was blowing huge green bubbles, popping them, and licking the gum into her mouth. Her eye makeup was much, much thicker and darker than he was used to on a girl. David suddenly wanted to reach out and pop one of the bubbles for her, but when he looked at his hands, they just stayed at his side.

"What about me?" David asked, and took a long sip of his beer.

"You play ball?"

"That's basically what I do, yeah."

"You'd fit right in in St. Louis," she said. "I—"

Kelli was cut off by a gigantic roar from the staircase above. It was a tearing sound, as if someone were trying to rip apart a couch using an electric saw. David and Kelli and a few others who had been getting beer went upstairs to see what it was. When they got to the parlor floor, they saw Mickey Pardo on a white Vespa.

He'd driven the scooter up the front steps, through the door, and into the living room, ripping apart a small entryway rug that was now lodged between the Vespa's back tire and the fender and currently catching fire.

"Wow," Kelli said.

David winced. After that "nice" comment about Arno, he could perfectly well imagine what was coming next. She'd walk over to Mickey. And it was right then that David felt the headlock of self-pity and attraction to girls that had pretty much defined every minute of the last several years of his life, save when he was playing ball. He didn't like Kelli. He missed Amanda, who was clearly avoiding him and he was freaking out, hard, about where she was. But when Kelli walked away from him, twitching her tight butt in that stupid skirt and sort of half-clenching her fingers, he thought, *she's hot.* And as usual, he felt bad and told himself that she'd only been killing time with him until a cooler guy came along.

"You're here," Mickey yelled to David. "Now where the hell is the rest of us?"

But David just ignored his old friend and yanked the hood of his sweatshirt over his head. Then he went and sat on a couch. He had another Heineken in his kangaroo pocket, and he got it out and opened it, found a straw and put it in. He sipped the beer through the straw and became invisible.

"Hi," Kelli said to Mickey. "What's your name?"

"Call me Stuntman Jack," Mickey yelled, and laughed. He stepped off the scooter, handed it to a freshman who'd been ogling it, and put his hands on Kelli's hips.

She said, "Ooh."

mickey pardo knows how to wake up a room

"Ooh?" Mickey asked. "Is that your name?"

"Keep making entrances like that and you can call me whatever you want," Kelli said. "Won't this kid's parents be upset that you drove a scooter into his house and set fire to the rug?"

The freshman, whose name was Adam, leaned Mickey's scooter against the wall. Then he threw beer on the flames until the fire went out and the rug began to smolder.

"Thanks," Mickey said, and nodded approvingly. An odor came up from it, something resembling burnt peanut-butter cookies.

"Nah, they won't care," he said. "Patch's parents are my dad and mom's oldest friends. They buy all my dad's art and stuff . . ."

Mickey looked down at the damage he'd done. He wasn't tall, and he was a little squat, like his father, Ricardo Pardo, the famous sculptor. He was wearing a green jumpsuit and black motorcycle boots. There were goggles and a whole bunch of Carnevale beads around his neck. A friend of his mom's had bleached his black hair blond, and now it had grown out all spiky, so his skull looked like it had sprouted match heads.

"Actually, yeah," Mickey said. "They might be annoyed. Have you seen Philippa?"

"I don't keep track of girls," Kelli said. "I came here with Jonathan." She followed Mickey as he made his way down to the kitchen. On his way, Mickey stopped for a second in front of David.

"You good?" Mickey asked, and tried to pull David's hood off. David slapped Mickey's hand.

"I can't find Amanda," David said.

"I'll take care of it," Mickey said. And that made David feel a little better, even though he knew Mickey would probably forget his promise in the next few minutes.

Meanwhile, other kids came up the steps and into the house, so what had been only twenty people was quickly becoming forty. They all carefully stepped around Mickey's stinking Vespa.

"Well, Ooh. Where did Jonathan find you?" Mickey asked. He slapped hands with guys and kissed girls on cheeks as they moved along, but he didn't try to lose Kelli for two simple reasons that floated through his mind: 1) she was a friend of Jonathan's, and 2) he could overlook certain aspects of her, like her ugly pink sweater, and feel the heat-seeking center of her, which was easy, because she was gripping his hand.

"We're cousins," Kelli said. "But he brought me here and ditched me the moment we walked in the door. Now I have no idea where he went. But that's okay, 'cause I've got you now."

"What'd you do to David Grobart?"

"Who's that?" Kelli asked.

"Damn," Mickey said. "I need to work with my man on how to make a better first impression."

"The hooded ballplayer? He's just like the kids back home."

Mickey didn't bother to ask where that was. He snagged a couple of del Sols from someone's six-pack on the counter and began drinking them. Kelli took one for herself.

"Listen, Ooh. I'm going to the roof for a sec. I can see my girlfriend Philippa's house from there and I want to try and figure out if I can like climb over there or something, since her parents are having a dinner party and I can't just go through the front door. So I'm thinking I'm going to go rooftop to rooftop. You want to come?"

"Sure," Kelli said. "You want to get some rope?"

"Nah, I won't need it," Mickey said. And he turned

and raced up the stairs. On the way, he knocked up against a girl with big dark eyes and black hair in a ponytail. A cool girl. Liza Komansky. Liza was with Jane Hamilton, whom she always took to parties. Jane was a wispy blond girl, tall, quiet, and widely known to be gay.

"Hey, Mickey, seen Jonathan?" Liza asked.

"Nah," Mickey said. "But this is his cousin, Ooh."

"Cousin It?" Liza said, and raised an eyebrow. Mickey saw Kelli slow down as she heard this.

"Ooh," Mickey said, and ran up the stairs.

Kelli stopped on the stairs to shake hands with Liza and Jane. The two girls gave Kelli the once-over. Liza was wearing black Gucci boots, a black Marc Jacobs knee-length skirt, and a matching black silk turtleneck. Jane was wearing blue jeans, engineer's boots, and a wifebeater T.

"I'm Kelli," Kelli said. "I think Jonathan went upstairs, but I can't find him." Kelli kept staring at Liza. Liza stared back. "Hey," Kelli said, "I really like your skirt."

"Thanks," Liza said.

"It's cool, but like in a really conservative, non-sexy way. Definitely wouldn't attract the wrong kind of attention, or any attention. Huh?"

"I hadn't thought of it that way," Liza said.

"If I wore something like that back where I'm from I'd practically disappear. But I guess people are more understated here in the city. I mean, I wouldn't be, but I can see how some girls might choose that road."

"Well, I suppose I did," Liza said.

"Yeah, that's what I'm saying." Kelli tugged her sweater up, so more of her belly was visible. And then she shrugged and smiled at Liza and Jane. "It's like I already forgot you," she said, and raced up the stairs after Mickey.

Liza Komansky watched Kelli go. From Liza's vantage point, the lines of Kelli's purple thong were visible. Kelli wobbled once and Liza stared at her cheap red pumps.

"That was unpleasant," Liza said to Jane as they watched Kelli go. They could just hear her make a whooping noise as she arrived at the top floor.

Jane looked contemplative. "She definitely has that cat eye thing going for her though."

"Sure," Liza said. "You know that completely overblown sexiness they taught Christina Aguilera in the Mickey Mouse Club? She's got it, too."

"I see you're not a fan." Jane stared after Kelli.

"I'm over it," Liza said. "Let's go find Jonathan."

i can't keep track of everybody!

"I'll see you later," I said.

"I'll be asleep later," said Flan.

I stroked her hair, just for a second, and then I said, "Oh, right." I tried to laugh. I absolutely would not call what I had on Flan a crush. I tried not to stroke her hair again but I couldn't help it. She smelled like clean sheets and flowers and cinnamon-flavored lip gloss.

"And I was having fun hanging out with you," Flan said. "So what if Arno saw us? Wasn't he fooling around with David's girlfriend? David needs to chill with her anyway. She's way too snarky for him."

"I know. But David shouldn't find out that they were together, not till he can handle it, anyway. Promise me you won't tell anybody about that."

"How will you know when he can handle it?" Flan asked. Her eyes were big and round and blue, like when you look at the earth from really far away. I sighed.

I tried to stand up and walk out of the room, but I was still stroking her hair. At that moment, although she was built like a *Sports Illustrated* swimsuit model, she had on a pair of floppy green-striped boy's pajamas that had probably belonged to Zed and slippers that had rubber-duck heads on the toes. She'd grown up so fast that her chest was about to burst the big white buttons off the front of her pajamas. And she didn't look tremendously upset about that.

"You two dressed yet?" I called out, low, to Arno and Amanda.

"No," they said back. There was the sound of clothes getting adjusted and then Amanda said, "I'm going down first."

Arno said, "I'm coming in there, and you better not have your hands on our best friend's little sister."

"Whatever, Arno," I said. "Let's get downstairs and figure out what's going on."

Arno came into the room. I'd been sitting in a sky-blue velvet chair that Flan had by the side of her bed, and I got up. Flan had been curled in bed, and she got up, too.

She said, "Can I get a beer?"

And Arno started laughing and I kind of did, too.

"No way," Arno said. "Bad enough we can't ever find your brother. We don't want to lose you, too."

"My sister lets me have beers."

"Yeah," Arno said. "Somebody should talk to February about that."

I gave Flan a quick kiss on the cheek and she sort of rubbed her nose on my nose in this heart-breaking sweet way she has and then me and Arno got out of there. We slid down the stairs fast, like we were on skis.

"Dude, you cannot fool around with an eighth grader," Arno said.

"I *wasn't*. I was just taking a break from all the craziness."

"Do not shovel me that bullshit," Arno said. "You're not new to me."

"I would bet anything I own that your universe is more morally fucked up than my universe," I said.

"You'd bet your shoe collection?"

"Don't be insane," I said.

"Hmm. How about if I win, no more Flan Flood

for you?"

I stopped for a second. Give up Flan Flood? I looked back up the stairs. It wasn't like I *had* her to give up, but I knew that a lot of the reason I liked the Flood house so much was because she lived there. It wasn't like we saw Patch nearly as much as we used to. We talked about him, sure, but we didn't actually *see* him.

"No way. I can't turn my back on her. She needs me." We slowed on the staircase when we came across Liza and Jane. "Hi, Liza."

"Hey, I met your sleazy cousin," Liza said. "And where've you two been?"

"Crossing swords in the upstairs bathroom," Arno said. He ran down the stairs, away from us.

Liza looked after him and shook her head. "He's headed in the wrong direction. All that's down there is David Grobart, and he's pulling a pity party for one. Mickey went in the other direction, upstairs, and he took your cousin with him."

"That's weird," I said. "I didn't see Mickey. I wonder how she got to him."

"It's not like that bitch is going to heel if you leave her alone."

"I thought you were over it," Jane said.

So we turned and raced back upstairs to the roof.

The Flood roof was something special. The usable area ran the whole length of their brownstone, and they'd covered it with trellises and all kinds of plants. There was a gardener who came every other day to make sure all the growing things kept growing and that the place looked extremely cool and kind of like a jungle, with all sorts of hidden areas and babbling brooks. Toward the end of the school year we liked to blow off days and go up there and hang, if we couldn't make it out to somebody's house in the country. At night, it got better. There was a fridge up there that we kept stocked with beers and cans of Red Bull and bottles of vodka.

We got upstairs and Mickey was screaming, "Philippa! Where are you?"

Philippa Frady had the same setup as the Floods, across the gardens, on Charles Street. Sometimes we yelled to her, and when we were younger, we used to toss water bombs and stuff onto her roof and into her garden. But that was all before she and Mickey became Romeo and Juliet. Her dad was some big investment banker who had invested in Mickey's dad's career early on and then they'd had this huge falling-out and were always fighting at the dinner parties all our parents can't stop having—the ones that inevitably result in somebody's parents not talking to somebody else's parents for six months or a year.

"Dude, she's coming over, can't you see her?" Arno said. He grabbed Mickey by the scruff of the neck and pointed his head down at the garden. Philippa was coming through her garden to the Flood house. They'd cut a hole in the wood fence back when we were in kindergarten and they'd just left it open.

"Philippa!" Mickey yelled.

"Hi, Jonathan," Kelli said. "You ditched me."

"Did I?" I asked. "I can't say that I did, no."

"I'm saying it," Kelli said. "Some cool city cousin you are."

There were half a dozen of us up on the roof. Me, Arno, Mickey, and then there was Kelli, Liza, and Jane.

"Where's Amanda?" Arno asked.

"Where's David?" Liza asked.

"Well, they go out," Kelli said. "Maybe they're together."

"How'd you know that, Ooh?" Mickey said. We all looked over at him. He was clambering over the side of the roof.

"I can get down with a scene very fast," Kelli said. She smiled and all of us looked at her. She was still in her pink sweater and white skirt, but she looked different than she had at dinner, more comfortable and sexy. Then she must've felt all our eyes on her—because she pointed at the place where Mickey had been, and he wasn't there.

"Mickey!" I screamed.

"Philippa!" he yelled. "I'm coming."

We heard him as he tried to scale down the trellis. Then we heard the trellis loosen from the side of the brownstone.

Liza called out what I was thinking: "Hey, Mick-head, why don't you take the stairs?"

Then we heard a whistling noise, and a thud.

david tries to get himself
and his girlfriend back on track

"What've you been up to?" David Grobart asked. He was with Amanda on the parlor floor, where all was relatively calm. He'd taken his hood off. Someone had put on some old Air and though nobody was dancing, the vibe in the room was good. David still had his seat on the couch and Amanda was next to him, but they hadn't been touching.

"Nothing," Amanda said. "What about you?"

"Well, first I couldn't find you, and so I hung out with Jonathan's cousin Kelli. Then she left and I couldn't find anybody."

"Me neither, I couldn't find anybody."

David sidled up closer to Amanda. He tried to work his arm around her back, but she wasn't having it.

"Don't cuddle me," Amanda said.

"I'm a cuddler," David said. He was using a voice that made him sound like Elmer Fudd.

"I know, but we're at a party."

"Be my Tweety Bird."

"Shut up!" She wriggled away from him.

Two years earlier, she'd been his fantasy. A short girl with long hair, Amanda had the distinction of being an even hotter version of Jessica Simpson, with the same blow-the-doors-down voice and a southern, take-no-crap attitude that she got from her mom, who had been a spokesmodel for NASCAR before marrying her rich dad.

"What's the matter?" David asked. "Seriously."

"David," Amanda said. She kept fooling around with the hem of her shirt, which was still damp from the upstairs bathroom floor.

"I—"

"What?"

"We need a stretcher!" It was Jonathan, running down the stairs with a red face. He grabbed David by the sweatshirt and pulled him away from Amanda, who was looking at the stairway, clearly waiting for someone else to appear.

"Mickey fell off the roof. Let's go," Jonathan said. He stared around. "Maybe only guys should come. This could be ugly."

Of course everyone ignored him. So with Jonathan, Arno, and David in the lead, they all ran down to the garden floor and streamed out the back, yelling Mickey Pardo's name.

When they got there, they couldn't find him. Finally, David looked up and there he was, cradled in the Floods' patio awning.

"You okay?" David called up to him.

Mickey made a flat, pained noise that basically signified that no, he wasn't okay, because he'd just fallen off a building.

"Anything broken?" Jonathan called.

"My arm. The rest of me bounced. Where's Philippa?"

"She called my cell just now," Liza said. "Her dad saw Mickey in flight and he pulled her back inside."

Then almost everyone began to wander back into the house.

"Let's get you down," David said. David and Jonathan got a ladder and pulled Mickey off the awning.

"That was one good fall," Mickey said. "I saw everything spinning—"

"Ow," David said. "Look at his arm."

They stared at Mickey's arm, which looked as if someone had stuck a softball where his elbow was supposed to be.

"We need to go to Saint Vincent's," Jonathan said. "David, you should come with me."

"But," David said. He made a gulping sound and

looked around for Amanda.

"Come on," Jonathan said. "Mickey's destroyed himself."

So David hung his head and got on one side of Mickey, and Jonathan got on the other.

"I broke my arm," Mickey said.

"Let's hope that's all you did," Jonathan said.

"Ow," Mickey said. "Don't yank me."

Kelli came up quickly and poured beer into Mickey's mouth. When he dribbled, she patted his lips with her fingertips.

"Mmm," Mickey said. "You're dreamy."

"Arno, you're coming with us, too," Jonathan said. He opened the door to the Flood house and the four boys stepped outside.

"What's up?" Arno asked. "You want me to come with you?"

They helped Mickey down the Flood steps and then stood in a circle on the street.

"I guess you don't need to," Jonathan said. "Stay here. Um, watch out for my cousin."

"Oh, I will," Arno said, and smiled. "Anything else?"

"Call us if Patch comes home," David said.

"Yeah, right." Arno said. "I haven't seen that dude all week. We should probably look for him, actually . . ." His voice trailed off and he looked back up at the dimly lit house. "Have a good time at Saint Vincent's. Buy some porn mags or something while you wait," and Arno bounded up the stairs and back inside.

The three of them looked up at the now-closed door.

"What's up with him?" David asked Jonathan. Jonathan just shrugged.

"I always feel like the moment I don't know what Arno's up to, that's not good," David said. "Like he's, like he's like the devil!"

Mickey started laughing and said, "We're friends with the devil!" Then he cried out in pain.

"Oh, stop it," Jonathan said as he hailed a cab. "If Arno's the devil, then I'm an angel."

"You're a fairy is what you are," Mickey said, and hung even harder off Jonathan's neck.

"Then get off me," Jonathan said.

"No way," Mickey said. "You're Glenda the good fairy."

"Screw you, Picasso," Jonathan said. "Ask the devil for help. I can see I'm not appreciated."

Jonathan let David take Mickey's weight, and the two of them fell against a parked Explorer and staggered, like a pair of old drunks.

"Okay, okay," Mickey said. "I take it back."

"You need to retire that jumpsuit," Jonathan said as

he helped Mickey and David stand up straight.

"Believe me," Mickey said. "The moment I'm ready to go clothes shopping, you'll be the first to know."

When the cab came, it was Jonathan who talked the driver into letting them get in.

liza and i do not discuss our past

Okay, I admit it. Even though I pretend I'm all good at keeping us together, I'm not a pro at it. I'm clearly not in control of everybody's destiny, since Mickey had ended up in the hospital and there wasn't a thing I could do about it.

So I stood in the waiting room at Saint Vincent's with Liza, who'd gotten bored at the party and had come to find us. She was on her knees, playing patty-cake with a five-year-old named Kevin whose mother had gotten out of bed and broken her ankle. I was on the phone to the Flood house, but of course nobody was answering. I tried Arno's cell, but he wasn't picking up either.

"I hope Kelli's okay," I said.

"What are you worried about?" Liza asked. "She's a big girl."

"You hate her?"

"That'd be like hating football season," Liza

said. "It'll go away soon, so why bother? They're keeping Mickey overnight?"

"Yeah. Let's go."

"Five minutes," Liza said. "Kevin promised he'd calm down once we finish our game."

So I had to wait while Liza finished with Kevin. And part of me wished she'd do the same for me, and another part remembered that Liza kind of had done that just last weekend.

We'd been at Patch's and I'd been blown out and she'd just brought me up to one of the bedrooms on the fourth floor and basically put me to bed. And that was when I got to talking to Flan Flood. I'd been lying there, staring at the ceiling and wondering how everyone was going to handle the night without me, and sort of filling in the blanks of who was going to do what and who was thinking what, like I always do, when Flan peeked into the room. I pretended to be asleep, so she came in and stared down at me.

"You want me to take off your shoes?" Flan had asked.

"No."

"Well, I don't think my parents would want them on their bed."

"These are pretty good shoes," I said. I

propped myself up on one elbow and looked at Flan. "I got them at Barneys. They're Jasper Fords, from London."

"Are you gay?" Flan asked.

"No. I'm just really into shoes. My friends are cool with it."

"Because they're gay." Flan sat down in a big white chair on what seemed to be her mother's side of the bed and she laughed.

"No they're not," I said. "Liza's friend Jane is. But I'm not, and neither is your brother or Mickey or David or Arno."

"The Insiders."

"Yeah, in fifth grade that's what I thought we were." I couldn't help sounding kind of nostalgic.

We ended up talking about how her clique wasn't a whole lot different from my clique. And then we heard people headed for the roof and I got nervous that they'd come in, but they didn't. So I tickled her for a while and then got out of there. But not before we kissed. Just once.

Back in the hospital, Liza finished her game. David had gone home a while ago. We'd called Mickey's parents, but they were out in Montauk at the farm where Mickey's dad made all his really big art. Nobody could remember the number out there, and I'd gone ahead and signed Mickey's bill onto my credit card, so we didn't have to worry about insurance or any of that complicated stuff.

Liza and I walked out into the night. It was nearly four and the air was cool, now that the rain had ended. The only cars on the streets were cabs and weaving sedans full of club goers headed down Seventh Avenue to the Holland Tunnel and back to New Jersey. I had to go east to my mom's place on Fifth and Eleventh Street, and Liza had to walk west, to her mom and dad's town house on Cornelia Street.

"I wonder how Kelli dealt with the party," I said.

"When we left, she was with Arno."

"I can imagine how that's going."

"Jonathan," Liza said. She was staring straight forward, into the street. We were a normal distance apart, but I could feel how she wouldn't have minded being closer to me. So I did get closer, but I didn't put my arms around her. We hadn't fooled around in six months or something. And when we did fool around it had just felt too appropriate, like that was something everybody expected us to do. I knew I wasn't excited enough to keep doing it. But I'd never said that. We'd just stopped fooling around, but we never stopped hanging out.

"What?" I asked. Maybe it's a double negative, when you know someone wants to say something, but you're too preoccupied with something else to deal with it. So you kind of . . . don't let them.

"Nothing," she said. "I hope you find your cousin."

I didn't like the sound of that, but it was too late to do anything, so I hugged Liza good-bye, told her I'd be in touch about tomorrow night, changed directions, and walked back to the Flood house to get Kelli.

"What'd Mickey call you?" Arno asked.

"Ooh," Kelli said. "I guess he thought that was funny."

There was a mirror above the mantel and Kelli looked at herself. She moved her white-blond hair around. Arno watched her do this, and then he checked out his own hair. "Like falling off a building for no reason is funny."

Kelli laughed. They locked eyes in the mirror. Music was still playing in the Flood living room, some soft stuff by Idlewild, and Arno wondered if Kelli had put it on. There were maybe five kids left, and Arno didn't know any of them well enough to care what they thought of him.

"You know, this place is kind of amazing," Kelli said.

"You should see my house," Arno said. "People call it the asylum."

"Why?"

"Because it's huge and crazy. My parents are art

dealers, so the public rooms are filled with lots of crazy art. Where are you from again? They probably help out with shows at the museum there."

"St. Louis."

"Oh yeah. I flew there with them. The stewardess was into me and so she took me to this special bathroom that only the staff uses. And that's when I joined the Mile High Club."

"Bullshit."

"For real," Arno said, smiling. Kelli was definitely hot. For instance, she could curse and it came out sounding like she wasn't imitating people who really cursed. She picked up a white marble vase. He watched the movement of her arms.

"I'd like to see the asylum sometime," Kelli said.

"I'd like that, too. Tomorrow night you'll come to the opening of a show I was involved in at my family's gallery. The artist is Randall Oddy; you might know his work. We'll start the evening there, and then if things go well, we'll end up at my house." Arno stuck out his hand and ran it under Kelli's chin. She gave him a sort of half smile and licked her upper lip.

"You're nothing like your jittery cousin," Arno said.

"I think I'm really going to like New York."

Arno walked backward away from Kelli. She followed him. He wasn't sure where he was going, and his interior map of the Flood house was not very good—not at nearly four in the morning, after a dozen beers. So he accidentally flipped over a couch. Kelli laughed so hard she nearly choked.

That's when the door opened and February Flood and her friends came in. Arno stood up.

"Arno, you idiot, what are you doing here?" February screamed out. "And who's this piece of trailer trash?" February wore dark eyeliner and darker clothes. Her short hair was in a bob, and her brown eyes were huge and glassy.

Kelli stopped laughing. February's friends crept around her and streamed up the stairs to her room.

"Where's my brother?" February asked.

"There's a question," Arno said. "I definitely haven't seen him all night. Meanwhile, Mickey fell off your roof so everyone took him to the hospital. What've you been up to?"

"Cheetah. We rocked it."

"Oh, did you?" Kelli said. She said "rocked it" under her breath, and shook her head.

"Listen, bitch," February snapped, "this is my house. I don't know who you are, but I think it'd be a good idea if you got out, now."

"Fine," Kelli said, and headed for the door.

"February, give it a rest. She's Jonathan's cousin.

Kelli, stay."

"Jonathan! Well, where the hell are you from, dressed like that?"

"St. Louis."

"Huh," February said. "You know, you two make a good couple. Arno, you're a total slick salesman, and you, you're . . ." But February didn't bother to finish the sentence. She was noticing that the house was trashed. She didn't seem bothered by this; she was just appraising the damage.

"Have you seen Patch?" February asked.

"You already asked that," Arno said. "We're going to hang out here for a while, okay?"

"These two can stay, but the rest of you get the hell out of here," February said, suddenly turning on the few other kids left on the parlor floor. The stragglers stood quickly and shot out the door like mice. February nodded to herself and went up the grand staircase, leaving Kelli and Arno alone together. Kelli put her finger on Arno's nose and pressed.

"You're pretty cute," she said.

"That's different from what you are. I would describe you as extremely hot." He took her finger in his hand. He put it in his mouth and said, "Come home with me now."

"You know, with Jonathan gone for who knows how

long, I would've done just that. But I don't think my mom'd appreciate it. Besides, he's at the door."

The front door opened and there was Jonathan, fighting to catch his breath.

"Hey," he said. "Kelli, we better get home."

"I want you over at my house tomorrow night, early, for cocktails," Arno said. He looked into Kelli's eyes.

"You're pushy," Kelli said. "I like that."

"We're—" But Arno caught himself before he said *meant for each other.* He was embarrassed that he'd thought it, because it sounded completely cliché unless you meant it, which he didn't. Of course, normally he didn't have to come up with smart lines. Normally, he just kept his mouth shut and got laid.

a breezy saturday in the city

mickey makes good use of his hospital bed

"Will you marry me?" Mickey asked.

"When I grow up, I can," Philippa said. "In like a year."

They dissolved into laughter. With his good arm, Mickey pulled her toward him. She'd shown up a little while earlier, in a white fleece jacket, Prada sneakers, and a Diane Von Furstenberg wrap dress. And once she was pretty sure Mickey was fine, she'd gotten up on his hospital bed and unwrapped.

Mickey had woken up a few hours earlier and stared out at the Saturday morning haze. He missed Philippa. He'd really broken some bones, too, but by the time she'd arrived and climbed on the bed, he figured out that they'd kept him overnight because they'd seen the psychotic episodes on his chart, not because of his arm.

Now Philippa, who had long, gangly legs and a moonface that didn't fit with them, big, pouty lips, and high, arched eyebrows, was sitting in the middle of his bed and playing a game with him. She kissed his nose and he tried to move quick, so he'd get a kiss on the lips instead. Mickey had taken off his hospital smock. Neither of them cared that they couldn't lock the door.

"I heard from Liza that Jonathan brought some gross relative of his last night and everybody was trying to get her bombed so they could sleep with her," Philippa said.

"It's your direct manner—that's what I love."

"You didn't do that, though," she said, and slowly pushed his broken arm back, above his head. She raised an eyebrow. Mickey held his breath. He knew that if she found out he cheated, she would break it again. Luckily, he hadn't.

"It hurts," Mickey said. And she bent over and kissed him. "Forget school. I'm going to stay in this bed till you marry me."

"I will marry you," Philippa said. "I said I would. Tell me more about Kelli."

"It's weird, I remember her as sexier than she actually is. Like somebody in a movie."

They were kissing when Jonathan walked in with cups of strong black coffee and a mouth that was so wrinkled and downturned that he looked about twenty-five.

Mickey pretended not to hear Jonathan, and so did Philippa. So Jonathan went to the window and opened one of the coffees. He got out his phone and called home.

"Hi, Mom. Did Kelli wake up? I just wanted to ask her something. No, don't bother. I'll be home later, probably. Yes, your dinner was wonderful and everybody was terrific and totally beautiful. Totally, yeah. Bye."

"I think someone's here," Philippa said, and laughed.

"Could you two not always be completely naked?" Jonathan asked.

"Don't look, then," Philippa said.

"I wasn't."

"That says a lot. Anyway, I've got to go to Sotheby's with my dad. He's bidding on a Lichtenstein against Arno's dad and he wants me to be there, to make sure I'm not spending time with this one." She gestured at Mickey.

"Your dad's so cheap," Mickey said. "Arno's dad is definitely going to win. You're around later?" He reached over to the steel stand next to the bed and grabbed a couple of pills and a cup of water. He took them, and his eyes fluttered.

"No, I've got to stick close to home tonight," she said as she pulled down her dress and tied it. "Call me later though, and tell me you love me."

And then she left.

"Let's go get lunch," Jonathan said. "Seriously. Put your pants on and let's get out of here."

Once they were outside and Jonathan had gotten Mickey to walk straight, they went over to the Corner Bistro and Bar, where the waiters knew them both because they'd been going there for after-school burgers since they were in sixth grade.

They settled into a booth in the back and ordered, and then looked around at all the hungover West Village fashion people, who were furiously chomping burgers.

"I'm looped on painkillers," Mickey said. He swung his broken arm over his head in circles, like a helicopter propeller.

"So you met my cousin before you flipped off the roof?" Jonathan asked.

"I didn't fool around with her."

"Well that's something. But you met her, right?"

"Ooh. Yeah . . ."

"Arno did."

"Got with her? How do you know?"

"I don't know what they did. But I left her with him for over an hour."

"Oh. Do you want to talk about how much I love Philippa? It's coming over me pretty hard."

"It's just annoying, that's all."

"Love?" Mickey asked. He bit into his burger. He sort of wished he could think of anything but Philippa. But he couldn't. Without her, what was he? He didn't know. He didn't always try to do crazy stuff . . . he just lost focus. He lifted his new cast up and down. Heavy.

"No, about Kelli. Arno always just fools around with everybody without any consideration for the consequences, or how it might make any of us feel. Did I even talk to you about what he did last night? He broke our code."

"What code?" Mickey asked.

"Um," Jonathan said. "Forget it." Mickey was just staring, as if someone were phoning over to him from another cloud. He looked around, with his head at a little bit of an angle. He didn't seem aware of himself at all. A waiter dropped off a couple of mugs of beer and Jonathan slid Mickey's out of his reach.

"That girl, Ooh," Mickey said, with his mouth full. "Hearing about her sort of flipped Philippa out."

"She's leaving in a couple of days."

"That's good. Philippa said that Liza wasn't that into her, and that's never a good sign." Then Mickey smiled the happy smile of a guy with a broken arm who is both completely in love and totally high.

i should have known better

I went home at four, after Mickey and I got ourselves fed, and I called around and arranged for all of us to meet for dinner at Man Ray at 8:30. There would be about eight of us: me, Mickey, David, Arno, Liza, Amanda, probably my cousin Kelli, and maybe Patch, though I hadn't spoken to him in days. I wondered what he was up to. This was getting to be the longest amount of time I'd gone without talking to him, and I definitely missed him. He had a calming effect on us all.

After I'd made the dinner plans I got to feeling hyper. I was supposed to read some play by Eurypides but it was Saturday afternoon—not exactly homework time. So I called Flan, since I figured she'd be home from her riding lessons.

I live right by the Floods, in a big old apartment building on the corner of Fifth Avenue and Eleventh Street, with about a dozen rooms that lead around and into each other like some kind of weird labyrinth, so when I'm feeling strange I just creep around with my eyes closed and try to figure out which room or corridor I'm in. And then I felt like that might be a game Flan would like. We could whistle and be blindfolded and bump into each other. And then I remembered I hadn't really had a chance to talk to her the night before.

"Let's go get ice cream," she said when I got her on the phone.

I was into that, because I love ice cream. So I slipped out of my Westons and into some very casual blue and white Prada boat shoes, and I wandered over to Otto, this new Mario Batali restaurant on Eighth Street, where they make ice cream by hand using old-fashioned butter churns. There she was, waiting in a booth by the window. And she was cute.

"Can we not sit by the window?" I asked.

"Are you afraid to be seen with me?" Flan teased. And then she stood up and reached across the booth and kissed me on the cheek. Which felt really good, and really, really wrong.

"Yes," I said.

"Shut up."

She kissed me again, and I could just see her looking at herself in the mirror, and it was like she'd rehearsed this moment at home this morning and that made my heart break a little more for her.

"How's your house?" I asked.

"You want to come back there with me and clean it up?"

"Uh-uh," I said. I got away from her and went to get our ice cream. I even knew her favorite flavor—cherry vanilla with chocolate chip cookies broken over the top. While I was paying I got a call from Liza.

"We all set for tonight?" I asked.

"Yeah, I got it. Man Ray, after nine. But I'm not sure how many of your boys can make it."

"What do you mean?"

"I hear that some people have other plans," Liza said.

"Who?" I asked. But she clicked off without answering, which is exactly the sort of thing she always does. I went back to our booth, juggling cell phone, ice cream, and change. Flan jumped up and took a cone from me.

"Jonathan," she said, once we'd gotten settled. "Where is this going?"

"What?"

"You and me. Where are we headed? You're

so bashful, but if we're going to go out, I need to tell people. For one thing, I'll need to find Patch and ask him if it's okay."

"Are you kidding?"

"I'm sure he won't mind, but I just want to tell him. Have you seen him?"

"No, and no. Look, Flan, this is like—I'm taking you out as like an interlude before I go out with my friends and stay out and party and do I don't even know what else yet—probably all night long. This is like my super-hallowed and innocent time before that happens, you know. I mean, I like you but you're young."

"No!" Flan said. "It's way more than that."

"No," I said. "It can't be."

She stared at me and her eyes got all full.

"Don't cry," I said.

"Why shouldn't I?" Her inflection was so right and charming. There was a lot of stuff I wanted to do right then that would've been more honest than what I did, which was to feel nervous and say nothing. She licked her cone a couple more times and then very carefully set it on a napkin on the table. Then she started breathing very quickly like she couldn't hold back real tears. Finally, she got up and ran out.

72

"Flan, wait!" I called. I whipped around and tried to follow her and immediately dripped ice cream all down my APC multistripe button-down. I ran out after her, but she was long gone—headed downtown, toward her house.

"Flan," I said. "Flan Flood. What am I going to do without you?" I couldn't believe I'd just said that. But there it was, and I had. I licked what was left of my raspberry peanut swirl and felt very sorry for myself, and all alone, and kind of pissed at myself for being completely unable to say how I really felt. And then I went home to change.

"You made it," Arno said.

Kelli smiled. Arno thought she looked even more Mickey-Mouse-Club-gone-bad than the night before, with her white-blond hair all flat and lanky, too much makeup, and her belly peeking out from above her tight jeans.

"Yeah," she said. "But I had to tell Jonathan I was going to hear Noam Chomsky speak at NYU about American imperialism before he'd leave me alone."

"Yeah," Arno said. "I do that all the time. Give us a kiss."

Kelli blinked at him.

"We don't really know each other," she said.

"Yeah?"

"You're right," Kelli said. "So what?" And she grabbed the back of his neck and pushed her body against him and kissed him. They were standing in the middle of Randall Oddy's show at the Wildenburger gallery in Chelsea, which was a huge white room about four times the size of the gym at Kelli's school.

For a while earlier in the afternoon Arno had thought that his Blackberry was broken, because it was going off so often with the same number, which turned out to be Amanda's. Finally, he turned the thing off. He'd been planning to do nothing all day but watch his bootleg *Matrix 3* DVD and he didn't want to deal with Amanda. Worse, he didn't even want to think about all his best friends being furious at him for doing the thing they'd sworn never to do, which was fool around with each other's girlfriends. But by the time Keanu had died for the third time, he'd gotten over it.

Now he was blissed out. Kelli was here. He had a simple plan. He was going to blow her away with the scene at the opening, and then he was going to take her back to his house and sleep with her. He didn't know what girls like her did back in St. Louis, but she certainly seemed willing.

"Let's go in the back," Arno said. He grabbed her hand and led her through the crowd, which was made up of hundreds of his mom and dad's friends and acquaintances.

"Arno, baby!" someone called out. Arno looked around. A tightly knit circle of young men and women opened up and a frenetically handsome young man in a black silk suit and a black T-shirt that said *Freaky* in yellow letters climbed through his admirers and made his way over to Arno and Kelli.

"Randall," Arno said. "Hot show. Very hot."

Arno swept his hands around and gestured at the walls. There were eight paintings of single eyes of very beautiful women caught in mid-wink, so that all the muscles were bulged out and terrifying. They were massive pictures and it took a second to realize what they were. Randall's last show had been of straining genitals, but he'd grown up a little since then, which was a relief to everyone who worked with him.

"Who's this?" Randall Oddy asked. He was staring at Kelli, who was staring back. Her lipstick was smeared from kissing Arno.

"Ooh," Kelli said. And Arno frowned.

"You two headed to the back room? Me, too—you two!" Randall said, and laughed. "Let me find a bottle of Cristal somewhere, and I'll join you."

"Great," Kelli said. "I dig your art."

"Maybe you can pose for me sometime," Randall said.

"I definitely want to do that." Kelli gave Randall a big wink. And as she did, her tongue came out of her mouth, and she used it to adjust her lipstick.

Arno sighed again, and in that moment, he felt something that he knew was far more familiar to guys like David Grobart, which was jealousy of Randall Oddy, a guy who might just be a hair cooler than he was.

As they walked back toward the sale room, Arno's Blackberry went off again. He took it out of his pocket and dropped it on the floor, and a model wearing heels that came to a point as sharp as a ballpoint pen stepped on it and killed it before suddenly falling down herself, like a capsizing sailboat. And Arno knew inside that right then poor Amanda Harrison Deutschmann, who was probably home all alone, getting ready to go out with her girlfriends, was sitting on her bed and crying, loud.

"Ooh," Kelli said. "This is even more fun than last night."

"Yeah," Arno said.

"I really like your artist friend. He's like the coolest guy I've ever met in my life."

"Kelli . . ."

"What?" She was looking around at the crowd. People stood in groups, with their backs to the paintings, telling stories and exchanging information on where to go later. Some were invited to the post-opening dinner for Randall Oddy, which would take place at La Luncheonette, over on Tenth Avenue. The rest would have to make do with smaller dinners of their own, where everyone would do nothing but talk about what was going on at the La Luncheonette dinner, which actually wouldn't be much fun, but they'd never know that because they weren't invited.

"What?" Kelli asked again, simply. Arno could see that Kelli was eyeing the outfits on some of the women and glancing down at her tight jeans and cheap black rayon blouse.

"You're so . . ." Arno trailed off. He'd been about to tell her that he really liked her, but then he caught himself. He guided her into the private sale room. A white bearskin rug was the only object in the room besides a couple of black chairs and a particularly pornographic Randall Oddy painting Arno's parents had hung on the wall.

He looked at Kelli. She was hot, sure, but that didn't mean he'd have to go caring about her or anything. Just 'cause she wasn't like anyone else he knew—so what? Wasn't nobody like anybody else? Hadn't he learned that in school? He closed the door and crossed his fingers, hoping that Randall Oddy had forgotten them and he could have Kelli all to himself.

"What a beautiful rug," Kelli said. She squatted down and stroked the fur and Arno stood behind her, looking at the foot-long jaguar tattoo that appeared when her shirt rode up.

"Cool tattoo."

"Yeah," she said, swiveling around to face him. "I got it when I was a freshman. It's our school mascot. Dorky, huh?"

"Maybe you'd like to lie down."

"On a rug like this, that's a really good idea," Kelli said.

"Hey, what's up, you two—are you going anywhere interesting after this?" Randall Oddy stood in the doorway, holding two bottles of Cristal and some plastic party cups. Arno and Kelli slowly stood up.

"It's your party, Oddy," Kelli said, making the two words rhyme.

"It's a party only if a girl like you is along for the ride."

"Huh," Arno said, low. He glanced over at Kelli, who had already forgotten all about the rug. Randall handed him a glass of champagne and they all raised their cups.

"What's the toast?" Kelli asked. She linked arms with Oddy and stared up at him.

"To us," Randall said. "Let's all hang out only with each other all night long!"

"I was just thinking how much fun that would be," Arno said, but he didn't smile.

david plays at the garden

"Come on, Davey, get your coat," Sam Grobart, David's father, said. "It's nearly seven and we want to see warm-ups, don't we?"

David slowly got off the couch in his apartment. He'd been pretending to play a game on his Blackberry—in fact he was trying to reach Amanda, which he'd been doing all day, so often that he'd had to lie about it to his parents, who tended to keep an eye out for addictive or destructive behavior.

"Why are warm-ups enjoyable to watch?" Hilary Grobart asked. In addition to being a therapist, she wrote her own line of self-help books, called *Always Ask First*, and so she was always asking first. David and her father sighed. It was like living with a paranoid parrot.

"We don't have to," Sam said, raising his voice. "But we *want* to."

"I see," Hilary said. "Come on, Davey."

The three of them stood up and David half-glared at his parents. They were immensely tall people, and handsome in a way, if they hadn't been so shy and awkward-looking, with their glasses and thick tweedy coats and responsible brown shoes. Every wall of their living room was lined with books, and everyone read all of the books all the time, so books were always teetering on the edges of the shelves, and they fell fairly often, so bunches of them lay on the floor with their spines broken.

In the elevator, Sam said, "We know you've been down in the dumps, but these seats are certainly going to cheer you up. I got them from Frederick Flood and they're right behind the bench."

"That's nice."

"He's a good man, but he ought to see his children more often."

"Isn't that confidential?" David asked.

"Because I'm his therapist?"

"Well, yeah."

"It is confidential, isn't it? Did you ask first?" Hilary Grobart said. David and his father sighed again.

Even though the Grobarts lived downtown in a big old apartment in the Rembrandt Building, on the corner of West Fourth and Jane, they walked briskly up to Madison Square Garden on Thirty-fourth Street. They walked everywhere briskly.

Along the way, David and his father talked about how incredibly lousy the Rangers were, and how it seemed as if they'd always be that way.

"But I don't understand, why are they so bad?" Hilary asked.

"Because Eric Lindros knows the inside of an MRI machine better than he knows his own ice skates," Sam Grobart said, and laughed at his own joke. His wife only shook her head and stared in complete confusion at some drunks who were fighting in front of the Wild Pony Bar on Twenty-eighth Street.

David thought of Amanda. They'd been dating for ten months straight, except for the summer, when she'd gone away to Turks and Caicos for diving school. She'd smoked so much pot down there that she'd e-mailed a warning to him that she might have irretrievably changed her personality and wasn't suited for him anymore. She'd sworn, though, that she hadn't fooled around with anyone, and that the only reason she hadn't called was that they didn't have phones. And then, when she'd gotten back in September, just a month ago, they'd had sex. It was the first time for both of them. Or so she'd said.

On that day, Labor Day, David had gone to Amanda's house in Tribeca, a gigantic loft that had been done up to look like an Upper East Side town house. He'd brought flowers and condoms and a bag of M&M's and shampoo. He'd read in a book that it's a sensual act if you wash a girl's hair. But when he got into Amanda's room, which faced the only airshaft in the loft and was decorated with the mid-century modern furniture her parents had been throwing away in favor of a more traditional look and a lot of horse ribbons that she'd won during summers out at their place in Sagaponack, Amanda just wanted to do it. He never even got the Infusium 23 with end enhancers out of the bag. Thus began what seemed like endless Tuesday and Thursday afternoons of sex (the days of no basketball practice).

He'd arrive with flowers or candy or nothing, and they'd dive under the yellow handmade Deke Fraternity quilt Amanda had been given by a group of admirers during a trip to visit her cousin at Duke, take off all their clothes, and work each other into a frenzy. Then when it was eight, David would go home and do his homework and Amanda would go out and meet her parents for dinner at Da Silvano.

"Let's call it love," David had said, on their third afternoon together. "I know I feel it, I'm in love with you."

Amanda had been lying on her side, faced away from him, flipping channels on the little flat-screen TV that was on her bedside table.

"Okay?" David asked. She turned over and glanced at him. She had the same placid look on her face that she had when waiters came to the table and announced the evening specials. Amanda's family were forever going out to dinner. It was the only thing they all really liked to do.

"Sure," she said. "I love you, too."

And David's world, which was already really good, got about a thousand times better.

"You want popcorn?" Sam asked, and prodded David in the ribs. David shook his head and let out a yelp. His dad's fingers were like gun muzzles.

"Come on, come on," Sam said as they got into the Garden. The Grobarts had used the Floods' Rangers tickets a few times before, so they knew their way to the face-on-the-glass seats, just a bit up and to the left of the visitor's bench. Tonight it was the Rangers against their archenemy, the Flyers.

They settled into their seats, with David on one side, then his dad, then his mom.

"Why is offsides called icing, and when does it occur?" David's mother asked. Sam leaned in to explain it.

David immediately began to text-message Amanda on his Blackberry. He wrote in long bursts, soliloquies, sonnets, great chunks of prose. He told her he'd do anything if she would just call, or send him back a note, or meet him later, or just somehow let him know that she still loved him.

"Jonathan, what the hell are those?" Mickey asked. He'd drifted into Man Ray on a dense cloud of painkillers. He looked down at Jonathan, who was slumped on the dark leather bench across from the bar, his feet up on a chair. Mickey grabbed Jonathan's ankle and pulled his foot up so he could better see what Jonathan was wearing in the dim light of the bar.

"They're from the new Saint Laurent line—something new that Tom Ford's trying out, imitation crocodile."

"They're orange loafers."

"Burnt sienna, actually," Jonathan said. "You're alone."

"And feeling no pain," Mickey said. He sat down and showed Jonathan his bottle of prescription Vicodin. "Want one?"

"No," Jonathan said. "You remember what happened last time."

Mickey nodded. Last time he'd let Jonathan use

drugs, they had been at a party on the Floods' old sail-boat out in Greenwich. Jonathan had taken the same thing as everyone else, but then instead of lying back and listening to music, he'd spent the next six hours running around counting the life preservers, and then counting the people on the boat, and then checking in with the coast guard to make sure no storms were coming even though the sky was the color of a baby boy's blanket . . . So, Mickey slowly withdrew the offer.

"Where's everyone else?" Mickey asked. He looked around the bar, as if Arno, David, and Patch might be hiding and were going to leap out and surprise him.

"They all said they'd be here," Jonathan said. Mickey grabbed the drink Jonathan was sipping and gulped it.

"Ah—what the hell is this?"

"Club soda with a splash of cranberry," Jonathan said.

"Jesus Christ," Mickey said. "I'm getting a beer."

He went up to the bar. Although it was Saturday night and just past eight, the place was quiet, even tomblike. The bartender was an extremely tall young woman in a black T-shirt and jeans.

"Could I get a Stella?" Mickey asked. He knew that even if he didn't know a staff member, they probably knew him. This was largely because he'd been coming to the restaurant for brunch with his parents since he was a little kid. The bar he was leaning against had been designed by his father before he'd gotten really famous.

The bartender looked in his eyes, which were as cloudy as his thoughts, and lined with red. She cocked her head to one side, then the other. Then she said, "No."

"What do you mean, no?"

"You keep nodding, but I'm not asking you a question. It's scary. So, no."

"Are you saying no because I'm sixteen, or because I'm on enough painkillers to knock out an elephant?"

"Yes," the bartender said. She pulled out a glass and the soda gun, poured Mickey a Coke, and handed it across to him. While this was going on, Mickey's attention drifted to the groups of people who were beginning to come through the door, all waiting for their parties to arrive so they could get seated in the back. He looked back at Jonathan, who was on the phone.

In all the darkness, Mickey realized he couldn't see the floor. There were just swirling mists down there. Part of him was grateful to the bartender for not letting him drink. The TV behind the bar was tuned to New York One, which was showing an interview with a woman who designed handbags shaped like dogs.

"Can we watch the Rangers game?" Mickey asked.

"If I say yes will you stay here so I can keep an

eye on you?"

"Yes," Mickey said back. "I want to keep my eyes on you, too." He was slurring. Then he frowned, and it was a clown's frown, big and sad and helpless. In about three seconds, the bartender melted for him.

"Gimme a kiss on the cheek and go sit with your friend with the funny shoes," she said. So Mickey reached over and kissed her and she smelled like whiskey and daisies. She reached out and tousled his thicket of matchstick hair.

"Do you think my girlfriend will be angry at me for being such a mess?" Mickey asked.

"Only if she finds out you kissed me," the bartender said. "Now get back to your friend. He looks upset."

"Can you believe it? I don't think anybody's coming but Liza," Jonathan said when Mickey sat down next to him. "And I don't even remember inviting her."

"Whatever," Mickey said. His arm felt like it weighed as much as one of his Dad's Cadillac sculptures.

"Where's my drink?" Jonathan asked.

By then Mickey was so zoned out that all he could focus on was the whizzing puck on the TV screen.

david gets the call

David smiled when he realized that he'd totally forgotten about dinner with everybody at Man Ray. That
was cool. He felt his cheeks glow. He never, never
forgot things, and always envied Patch Flood for being
so mellow that he could never be counted on to show
up for anything. And now here David was, casually at a
Rangers game with his parents, which was pretty cool if
you looked at it from a certain laid-back perspective
that David knew he didn't have himself but that some
of his friends did.

"They scored!" Sam Grobart yelled. He grabbed
David and they stood up and threw their hands in the air.

"What led up to that?" David's mom asked. Sam sat
down to explain.

So now the Rangers were one goal ahead and David
felt happy. It was the beginning of the third period and
all they needed to do was hold on. The smell of sweat
and beer hung heavy in the cold Madison Square
Garden air. And always, always he had Amanda in his

head. And he thought, *maybe she's just busy with her parents, at one of those five-hour, seven-course dinners.*

Then his phone rang and he grabbed it so hard that for a moment he flashed on a fear that it would squeeze out of his hand and fly onto the ice and be sliced in neat halves by one of the player's skates. But he got ahold of it. Saw it was Amanda.

"Hey, where've you been?" David asked.

"David, where are you?"

"That doesn't matter, at the Rangers game. What's going on? I've been trying—"

"I know you have," Amanda said. "There's something I need to tell you."

"What?" David asked. He scooted his head down between his legs so he could concentrate. The concrete steps were close to his face, and the air was dank.

"I don't know if we should be together anymore."

"What? Why?"

"I don't want to tell you. It'll make things terrible for everyone."

"What will? What are you talking about?"

"Don't push me, David."

"Push you?" David looked around—something was going wrong on the ice, too.

"You're forcing me to say it—I fooled around with someone else. You sort of know who the person is and

I'm not sure I even wanted to, and now I'm sick about it."

"What? Who was it? No!"

David dropped the phone. A cry escaped from his lips. Since he'd been in fifth grade and Arno French-kissed Molly, the girl David had been passing notes to, he'd been afraid a girl would cheat on him. And because of it, he'd been unable to have a girlfriend for all of middle school and high school all the way up to now. The shock of betrayal shot through him and he felt a slackening, as if he'd lost control of his body. He couldn't even begin to wonder who she'd fooled around with.

Then he was yanked to his feet. A massive, collective *no* erupted from the crowd. And David's dad wanted his son standing with him. Meanwhile, David was crying in pain. A moment earlier, a defenseman had checked a Flyer into the glass in front of the Grobarts. The guy pawed at the glass for a second before sinking to the floor.

Penalty! A power play!

A camera zoomed in on the fallen player, the screaming fans, the probability that now the Rangers would blow the win. Then the cameraman panned up a foot to David, who looked just like the sort of fan who equated a loss for his beloved team with something like getting a call from your beloved girlfriend, who says that she fooled around with someone you know. David had the face that said it all. *No!*

what happens when a girl likes you and you don't like her back enough

"Oh my God," I said. "Look at the TV." I stood up fast and part of my drink spilled down my pant leg.

On TV, a Flyer had been checked hard and the Rangers had basically blown the game. We'd watched this passively. I couldn't care less about hockey and Mickey seemed to have left the planet. But then there was a full screen shot of one very unhappy fan, who had gone from a shocked look of anger to a bout of tears. The camera lingered for a solid one, two, three seconds. The boy was bawling.

"That's David," Mickey said. He looked as if he were trying to slap away the cotton balls that were swirling in the air around him.

"Yeah, that's David, and he's crying. On TV," I said.

"I guess he's not coming to meet us," Mickey said.

"I wonder what the hell happened."

"He must've forgot."

"No, idiot—to make him cry like that, on TV."
But of course I knew. And I snarled inwardly at
Arno and wondered how I was going to fix what
he'd done. And Patch? Where was he? But there
wasn't time to worry about him then, not with
David crying on ESPN.

I sat there next to my doped-out friend, my
arms folded over my chest, and I puffed out my
cheeks and blew hot air. I glanced at Mickey. He
was making a kiss-me face and the bartender,
incredibly, was responding with a kiss-me face of
her own. Or she was making fun of him. It was
difficult to tell. Mickey unzipped his jumpsuit and
he had nothing on underneath. Some girls who'd
just come in with dates stared and Mickey stood
up and tried to dance for them, but he was too
messed up, so he sat back down, more on me
than on the bench. I pushed him off.

Sometimes I forgot just how much girls could
get into Mickey. They liked him because he was
shocking and exciting. Because he was crazy. I
wondered why girls might like me. Because I
know the difference between cordovan leather
and calfskin? Probably not.

"This night is thrashed," I said. Mickey's head was doing a first-rate imitation of a bobblehead doll.

"You should go home," I said.

"Why?"

"Look at you, you need rest. Otherwise you're going to miss school all week. Where's your Vespa?"

"I don't know . . . at Patch's?" Mickey smiled at me.

"I'll call you a cab."

"No," he said. "I can walk. I had no idea David was so into the Rangers."

"Yeah, me neither."

I glanced around and saw Liza come in the door, alone. She was in her usual all-black outfit, and her hair was pulled back. The older guys in the bar gawked at her. When Mickey saw her, he rose unsteadily to his feet and used the hug he gave her to keep himself up. She grabbed his face in her hands and looked in his eyes.

"Look, it's your girlfriend," Mickey said.

"No she's not," I said, too fast. Just because Liza and I hadn't gone out with anyone else last year, and had made out sometimes and talked on the phone most nights, people assumed we were going out.

"Go home," Liza said. "Please."

Liza took Mickey out to put him in a cab, and I used the time to call Flan Flood.

"Jonathan?" Flan asked.

"Are you doing anything?" I asked.

"Watching *My So-Called Life* DVDs with Laura and Rebecca. We know all the lines by heart. But we actually flipped by the Rangers game for a second and saw your friend David bawling like a little baby."

"Listen, I'm sorry about today."

"Oh, that's okay. Whatever." And I could hear her quickened breathing, and I knew she was just saying that because she had two friends over.

"Do you want to come and meet me?" I asked. But I saw the door open, and Liza was headed my way. And what was I asking Flan to meet me for anyway?

"I don't know if I can," she said, in her mature voice.

"You're right. You shouldn't. That was crazy of me. Look, I'm being really crazy. I'm sorry. You should ignore me."

"Call me tomorrow," she whispered, and ended the call. I looked up at Liza, who was standing over me.

"Where's the rest of your crowd?" she asked.

"Not coming. You want to have a drink? Who're you with?"

"I'm alone," she said. We went over to the bar. A deejay had set up in the corner and he'd begun to spin a remix of the Humpty song. We crammed ourselves into a tiny space at the bar and Liza ordered cosmopolitans for both of us. I tried to find something to say to Liza that didn't include the fact that I was becoming obsessed with a kid who watched old TV shows with her friends on Saturday night.

"My group is falling apart," I said.

"Where's Kelli?"

"I don't know. She was going to meet us here. I gave her a map and everything. Either she's lost or she got a better offer."

"And Arno blew you off, too."

"Yeah, those two are probably together somewhere, licking ice cream and chocolate sauce off each other." I tried a laugh, which came out sounding like I was choking on a chicken bone.

"Or they're just having sex."

"I was kidding," I said.

"I wasn't."

"Sometimes you're a little too blasé to deal with."

"That's only 'cause you're so naïve."

"Thanks a lot!" I said, and maybe I said it a little loudly because a table full of people looked over. But they were all old, past thirty, so who cared? I knew that Liza had much, much better things to do on a Saturday night than chase after me and my guys, and that led me to knowing that she expected something from me that I didn't want to give. But I couldn't change how I felt. I didn't want to be with her in the way I was last year, if it wasn't going to be genuine.

"This is one of those nights that's so awful that it makes me wonder why I live at all, you know?" I said. "Let's just go."

"Fine," Liza said. She'd barely touched her drink.

We began the slow walk home. Both our phones rang, but we ignored them. Saturday night was just heating up and the streets were busy. We passed Inca-Eight, a new club that had taken over the space where Suite Sixteen used to be, and even though the bouncers smiled at me and Liza, neither of us suggested that we should check it out.

"I should get over you," Liza said.

"Um," I said.

"I know I sound matter of fact about it," she said. "We were never wild enough together. And that was part of the problem, right?"

"I guess." I was never sure, though, what the problem was exactly. Everyone else thought we made sense together.

We got to her street and she kissed me goodnight on the cheek and we stared at each other. Then she shook her head quickly and ran up her steps. And all I could yell after her was, "Let's talk later!" Which was pretty funny when you thought about it, because we'd already said everything we'd been needing to say.

arno's night goes on forever and ever

"Now this is what I call a good time," Randall Oddy said. He sat between Arno and Kelli on a black leather couch at Ringo, a new club on Little West Twelfth Street that was run by Ringo Starr's stepdaughter Francesca in the basement of her town house. There were only forty people allowed in the club at any one time, and right then there were forty-one, including Francesca, who was playing old Beatles songs on the sound system, drinking absinthe, and chewing on the sleeve of a shirt that belonged to an eighteen-year-old soap opera actor who was passed out next to her.

Kelli was drinking a pint can of Miller Lite that she'd bought at the corner store. She didn't appear tired, or bored, or anything. Arno was staring at what he could see of her from around Randall's sparrowlike chest. Randall was staring at her, too. They were both fighting back yawns. It was 4:45 A.M.

Kelli pouted her lips, which she'd painted a pinkish white in the bathroom an hour earlier when she'd run into the model Jamie King, who'd bought Kelli's ankle bracelet off her for five hundred dollars. Now Jamie waved across at them from another couch on the other side of the room. But they could barely see her in the darkness—the whole place was done up in black leather and black velvet and all the lights were swathed in black silk. So except for the occasional flash of jewelry, it was really dark.

"I wonder where Jonathan's house is in relation to here," Kelli said. She dragged her fingers through her hair.

"You don't need to go back there," Arno said. She looked around Randall to see him.

"Why not?"

"You can stay with me," Arno said.

"Or we can just stay out all night," Randall said. "And we can all crash at my suite in the Mercer in the morning."

"I'd really like to see the Mercer," Kelli said.

"It's just a stupid trendy hotel," Arno said. Then he stood up. He didn't mind competing, but he felt like Randall should back off. After all, Kelli was only seventeen and Randall was in his mid-twenties. "And I saw her first!"—that's what he wanted to say to Randall. And he also wanted to say that he was going to complain to his dad when he saw him next and then his dad wouldn't give Randall any more shows and Randall wouldn't be a famous artist anymore. He was also considering punching Randall in the face. It was an awful lot of feelings, he knew, all for Jonathan's cousin from St. Louis.

"Hey, come sit next to me," Kelli said. As Arno settled in, she said, "I could feel how you were wanting to go home. Please don't leave me with Oddy."

She was warm and smelled like artificial fruit flavoring and baby powder. She held out her beer and Arno sipped from it.

"You won't leave me, will you?" she asked.

"No," Arno said.

Kelli put her arms around Arno and Randall.

"You two're my favorite guys in New York so far," Kelli said. "Except for my cousin Jonathan and that crazy guy Mickey and that quiet loser David who reminds me of the boys back home."

She kicked her legs in the air and laughed.

"I'm going to South Beach in the middle of the week to do some press and attend my opening down there," Randall said to Kelli. "Do you want to come?"

"I'm already taking her," Arno said quickly.

"Whooo-hoo!" Kelli yelled. "South Beach, with both of you! This is the best trip out of St. Louis I ever had." Randall and Arno turned and glared at each other, their arms folded.

Arno's extra phone kept buzzing with calls from David and Jonathan and Amanda, but he didn't notice because the phone was in his jacket, which was crumpled up on the floor at his feet.

"Let's go to Florent and get some breakfast," Randall suggested.

"Great, I love that place," Arno said.

"Fun!" Kelli said.

Randall laughed and Arno thought the noise was maniacal, and he tried to catch Kelli's eye so she'd agree with him. But she was already following Randall up the velvet-covered staircase.

Arno leaped up and ran to catch them.

the crash known as sunday

my quiet sunday morning

Sunday found me drinking black coffee in the kitchen at one in the afternoon and glancing at the already heavily picked-through Sunday *New York Times*. I hate the Sunday *Times*. It weighs about seven pounds and everything in it is dorky and wrong. Back before my dad moved to London, we used to read it together and he'd outline every single thing that the *Times* had misunderstood about business and the rest of the world. That was a little exhausting, but it was also pretty funny. So I went ahead and gave him a call to see if he wanted to talk about how stupid the paper was over the phone, but he wasn't home, or he wasn't picking up.

Then I spied something particularly insane and exciting. *Men's Fashions of The Times*. The magazine section. I knew for a fact that once I opened it my gut was going to hurt from laughing so hard at the assinine outfits those fools put together and called fashion, so I set it aside and decided to call around and see what had happened to everybody the night before.

I started with Arno. He picked up, which meant he thought I was someone else.

"I really don't appreciate you not showing up where I invited you and then taking my innocent little cousin and doing who knows what with her."

"Cool it, Jonathan," Arno said. "I just got home and you sound like my mom."

"Oh yeah? Well has your mom been asking you how far you got with my cousin? And did you see David crying on TV last night? He must've found out about you and Amanda."

"Maybe he was just into the game."

"Yeah, right. For your sake, you better hope that Amanda didn't tell him what she did with you."

"Yeah," Arno said slowly. "I guess I do hope that."

"Now what about my cousin?"

"What do you care?"

"Um," I said. And then I immediately realized that 1) I couldn't be jealous, because she was my cousin, and 2) Arno had fooled around with

Amanda and potentially destroyed David's relationship, thus violating the single pact we'd had going since we were tiny, or at least since fifth grade when Arno had French-kissed Molly, who had been passing love notes with David for practically the entire year. How was I going to keep us together if David found out what Arno did? Patch could probably mellow us out, but where the hell was he? I didn't have a clue.

"How could you do that to David?"

"Ask Amanda. It was her idea and believe me, I don't feel good about it."

"Hmm," I said.

"Listen, you're not going to tell David, are you?" Arno asked.

"No," I said flatly. "It'd kill him." And we hung up.

Then I called David, who didn't answer. I called Mickey, but he didn't answer either, so I gave up. The chances of Mickey knowing where his phone was were about as good as there being a decent pair of shoes on a model in the *Men's Fashions* section.

I sat there, spinning my phone on the kitchen table and wondering what to do with myself. Then I opened the magazine and started looking at the pictures of bunches of guys wearing ugly Wall Street suits with boring old white button-down shirts.

That's when I heard a noise and remembered that my house had visitors. Kelli wandered into the kitchen. To say she was unsteady on her feet was an understatement. She gripped the kitchen counter like it was the side of a sailboat and our apartment was the sea.

"Need something?" I asked. I tried to make my voice surly, but it didn't come out right. Even hungover as she was, she was a pretty sexy looking character. Her lips were puffy and pink and her hair was pointing in all directions. She didn't have bed-head. She had orgy-head.

"Back to bed, going," she said. "Mom?"

"Our moms are out shopping at Bergdorf's."

" 's lucky."

"Mmm," I said. "Out late?"

"Till just now," she said.

"Ready for your Barnard interview tomorrow? Coffee?" I asked. I poured a steaming cup and held it, just out of her reach.

"Mmm," she said. She reached toward it. I handed it to her and she needed both hands to steady the cup. She let go of the counter and trembled. When the coffee aroma reached her nose, she dropped the cup and vomited, instantly and heavily, all over our onyx Bizazza kitchen tile. Then she collapsed in a heap of platinum blond hair, makeup, and scuffed high-heeled boots.

She was asleep in a matter of moments. I grabbed a napkin and tied it over my mouth so the smell wouldn't kill me.

mickey and his dad sometimes disagree

"What the hell happened to you?" Ricardo Pardo asked his son, Mickey. His assistants were just finishing unloading the black Mercedes wagon he'd driven back into the city, and he looked at his son with a mixture of appreciation and complete disgust. Mickey swayed in front of his father. He was in a black cashmere bathrobe and combat boots.

"I have to repeat myself?" his father asked.

Mickey considered a lie, but the truth always got his father off his back quicker. Ricardo stared at his son. They were about the same height and looked terribly similar, except that Ricardo had a big belly and a thick black and white beard that came down to his clavicle.

"I climbed off Patch's roof to get to Philippa and fell," Mickey said.

"Say what?" Ricardo whipped around. Two of his assistants who were carrying boxes full of paint cans backed away in fear.

"You heard me," Mickey said.

"Hello, darling," his mother, Lucy, said. She'd taken her own Mercedes back from Montauk. She was a beautiful woman—a former model from Venezuela, and the fact that Mickey had inherited equal parts of his father's swarthy, froglike looks and his mother's stunning beauty was a source of amusement to everyone who knew the Pardos.

"Where's Philippa, darling?" his mother asked.

"Her dad won't let her speak to me."

"You know, *mijito*," his father said, "if hanging around with your buddies is going to get you nearly killed, then maybe that's over, you know?"

"Say what?"

"You heard me, *mijito desobediente!*"

"You're nuts, Dad!"

"*Chiflado?* You think so? No more Philippa for you, *hijo!* I agree with that Jackson Frady. You're driving us both *loco!*"

Ricardo and Mickey glared at each other. So Mickey jumped back and slammed the door to his bedroom, turned around, and threw himself on his bed. Or rather, threw himself where he *thought* his bed was. But as he felt the hard waxed concrete of the bedroom floor crunch against his elbow, he remembered that he'd rearranged the room in a fit of drugged ecstasy the day before. Taken all the rugs and soft things and put them in a big box in the corner.

"*Oww,*" he groaned.

the school week, which can't be helped

too late for david and amanda

David walked out of school on Monday afternoon with his head hung low. Earlier, his science teacher had wondered aloud if he'd broken his neck. He had a date to meet Amanda at Silver Spurs. He planned to arrive early and order a strawberry milk shake, on the off chance that the sugar rush would make him happy.

"Have a good night, crybaby," somebody yelled out.

"Hey, everybody make way for the most sensitive guy in the world!" a freshman on the hockey team yelled.

David knocked the kid out of his way without looking up. The guys from the hockey team had, of course, seen the Rangers-Flyers game. And his own guys from the basketball team hadn't bothered to defend him. The whole thing was worse than embarrassing. It would become school lore, the kind of story that would maybe even get its own page in the yearbook.

He slung his messenger bag over his Potterton Basketball jacket and headed for the diner. On the way, he punched in #3 on his cell after Mom, and Amanda, and Jonathan picked up.

"Are you ready for my advice?" Jonathan asked, after hearing David's story about what Amanda had done, which of course was a completely different story than what Jonathan had actually seen with his own two eyes.

"I'm ready."

"Break up with her before she breaks up with you."

"Why would I want to do that?" David asked. He stopped short in the middle of Bleecker Street and a cabdriver screamed at him in Farsi, which David knew, slightly, because of a trip he'd taken to Iran the previous summer with his parents. So he apologized, in Farsi. The cabdriver said to forget it before driving off.

"She cheated on you."

"But I love her."

"Look, you've got to be strong."

"I do?" David asked. He was close to the restaurant now. The dangling Silver Spurs logo hung in front of him like a pair of Amanda's gigantic earrings.

"Tell her to go to hell."

"No way!"

"It's the only way," Jonathan said, before David hung up on him.

David had seen Amanda slip into the diner, her mouth in a frown. She was so short and he was so tall.

He shook his head. They could have been so perfect. He sighed and opened the restaurant's door.

"What are you getting?" David asked. He'd sat down with Amanda and now they both looked miserable.

"Grilled cheese with bacon and tomato," Amanda said. She was always ordering stuff like that and then taking only two bites and pushing the plate aside. The booth they'd gotten was by the door, which kept opening and shutting, letting cool air in. This increased their shuddering. A waitress came by and dropped menus on the table before walking away.

They stared at each other, and David knew he was doing what he always did, which was getting blown away by how pretty she was, with her long blond hair and piercing green eyes.

"Who was it?" David asked.

"I don't want to say," Amanda said. "I'm not sure it meant anything. Maybe it did. Maybe it didn't."

"I don't want to see you anymore."

"What?" she asked.

"You heard me. You cheated on me, I can't trust you. It's over." He stood up and his legs felt like they were made of potato salad. But he knew Jonathan's advice was right.

"David, wait—"

"I can't. I know what happened isn't anybody's fault

and I don't blame you, but I can't see you anymore."

"You're being unreasonable." There was a quaver in her voice that felt unfamiliar to him. Maybe she really did care about him? He'd never dared to believe that before. And now it was too late. Then she stood, too.

"Forget it," David said. "I loved you."

Then he was out the door, walking fast away from her, west, toward his parents' apartment building, desperately trying not to think about what he'd done.

is my cousin an evil person?

"How'd it go?" I asked. I was standing in the doorway of my brother's old room. Kelli was packing a small bag and prancing around.

"How'd what go?"

"Your Barnard interview, stupid."

"Oh." Kelli turned around and smiled at me, in that kind of sickly sweet slutty way she had. She was chewing furiously on what smelled like Bubblicious. She blew a bubble at me. She was probably using three pieces.

"It was totally cool," she said. "We talked about art, mostly."

"Art?"

"Yeah, what's happening on the scene here in the city. Who the hot young artists are, what we can expect in the future, that sort of thing."

"No kidding." I looked down the hall, searched for a hidden camera crew or something.

My mom was up at Canyon Ranch in the

Berkshires with Kelli's mom for Tuesday and Wednesday and Thursday. So we were alone in the apartment.

"What do you know about art?" I asked.

"Not much," she said. "But I'm a fast learner."

She was packing some of her clothes into a leather Polo overnight bag that belonged to my brother.

"Listen, I'm flying down to South Beach in a couple of hours with Randall Oddy. Would you cover for me if my mom calls? Tell her my cell died and I'm in the bathtub so I can't take the call 'cause I don't want to get electrocuted."

I realized that was my mouth was open, so I shut it.

"You think that's not a good excuse?" she asked. "Tell her I've fallen in love with a mad talented young artist and I've decided to throw away my future in order to become his muse."

"Wait, didn't Arno invite you down there?" I asked.

"Yeah, he'll be there, too. I might stay with him. He doesn't know it yet, but he'll do anything for me." She was putting on bracelets, what seemed like a lot of them, and then she checked her shirt, and looked as if she wanted to change it. I didn't move. She shrugged and slipped off her shirt, so she was wearing only a tiny black lace bra. She said, "Don't be creepy. We're cousins. Anyway, sometimes when I meet people, they just fall for me instantly; it's a thing I have."

I turned around and looked at some boring photograph of lightning we had in our hall, in order to not totally check Kelli out.

"I doubt he'd do anything for you," I said. "And he didn't fall for you the moment he saw you. Half an hour after he met you, he was making out in a bathroom with Amanda Harrison Deutschmann."

"Really," Kelli said. "So he's the kind of guy who fools around with his buddy's girlfriend. That's interesting to know."

"I was kidding," I said quickly. "You're right. He'll do anything for you."

Kelli turned around and smiled at me.

"Yeah, right," she said.

"Kelli, don't tell anybody what I just said. I didn't mean to say it."

"Oh, you can trust me. Now could you get out of here? I need to overhaul my outfit so I'll look kick-ass for this trip."

"Damn," I said. And shook my head. "The devil really can take any form." I backed out the door and shut it. I walked slowly backward down the corridor and got myself into the relative safety of my own room. When I closed the door, my cell was ringing, thank God.

"I'm bored," Liza said.

"Me, too. There's absolutely nothing going on."

"Yeah, right. You want to go to Other Music and buy CDs?"

"Does this mean we're cool again?"

"Forget the other night," Liza said. "I'm over you. And I'm supposed to read *Madame Bovary* in French and I'm not really up for that right now, so come out and meet me."

I wasn't sure I believed Liza, but I went downstairs to see her anyway, without saying good-bye to my cousin, who was on the phone to someone, saying something about how much she loved the power of mixing film and art. Man. Next thing she'd be directing features and hanging out with Sofia Coppola.

"Any good gossip?" Liza asked, once we'd reached Broadway and been swept up in the crowd of NYU students and tourists.

"No," I said quickly.

We went into Other Music and started flipping through the "IN" section. Sometimes I looked through the "OUT" section, which could be much, much cooler than the "IN" section, because it was filled with stuff nobody was going to know about for another three months, but I just didn't have the energy right then. I was also kind of afraid I'd find some CD with Kelli's picture on the front.

"How do you know when someone's a really bad person?" I asked. They were playing the new Flaming Lips, and I hummed along.

Liza smiled. She was going through everything by Cat Power. Chan Marshall was her favorite person, and Cat Power was her favorite band.

"Since arriving in high school, I've asked myself that many times," she said.

"And what've you come up with?"

"If they lie to you, they're not very genuine. Everything else is splitting hairs."

We leaned against the "French Decadence" section and watched a ninth grader in a black leather jacket shoplift the new Interpol CD. He was a far-too-cool kid named Adam

Rickenbacher, and he went to school with David. I'd seen him hanging around the Flood house once or twice and I wasn't into him. He palmed an old Sonic Youth CD and took that, too.

"So what do you do?" I asked. "If someone lies?"

I nodded at Adam Rickenbacher and he nodded back. *Hey yourself, you little bastard.*

"Try to trust a few people at a time," Liza said. "And keep your fingers crossed."

"I wish my cousin would go back to St. Louis," I said. "She's freaking me out."

"I wish she would, too," Liza said. "Anyway, do we have to talk about her?"

"What else should we talk about?" I asked. I looked at her and then it was obvious. She wanted to talk about us, and I had nothing to say.

"I heard that David broke up with Amanda," she said.

"Oh yeah?"

"So I was thinking that I'd go out with David. The reason I called you is I was wondering, would you care?"

Not unless you were Flan, I thought. And then I felt suddenly sure about Flan, who I'd promised myself I wouldn't go near, and really bad about

125

Liza, who seemed to be able to tell from my face that she didn't want to hear my response. I was kind of shocked at my own feelings, so I looked at my hands, which didn't help. They were trembling.

Then, WOOOwooWOOOwoo—the alarm at the door went off and several of the balding/shaved-head Other Music employees went running after Adam Rickenbacher.

"That kid's got something going for him," Liza said.

"Give me a break," I said.

"I guess I will, from now on."

"You're not going to go out with David, are you?"

"Nah," Liza said. "He's too sweet for my taste."

Liza and I ambled out of there.

mickey gets to see his forbidden philippa

"You are not the most sensitive guy in the world!" Mickey said to David. They stared at each other for one very sober moment and then Mickey started laughing. It was Tuesday night and they were standing in front of Philippa Frady's house.

"I mean, that's pretty funny when you think about it," Mickey said. "There's people that'd kill for that title, probably. So if you see it in a certain way, it's cool."

"What are we doing out here anyway?" David asked miserably.

"Philippa said she'd show me a sign from her room if she wasn't in trouble anymore."

"What's the sign?" David asked.

"Her, without her shirt on."

"What about me seeing?"

"Cover your eyes."

Then the two of them were very quiet, staring up at the windows on the third floor. David had his hands over his eyes and he was peeking through his fingers.

Mickey knew he was doing this, but it didn't bother him. Mickey and Philippa didn't care if people saw them naked.

"What happened with Amanda?" Mickey asked.

"Jonathan told me to break up with her, so I did it."

"If he told you to—"

"To jump off a building? No, dude, I'd call you and you'd do it."

"You totally love her, don't you."

"Yeah," David said. "And now she's not speaking to me."

"How long?"

David checked his watch. Mickey kept his eyes on the window. He'd never cared much for Amanda anyway. She was too full of it. That's why he was with Philippa. They had a primal thing going.

"Thirty hours now," David said. He looked over at Mickey, who hadn't been in school for two days and was now looking incredibly bonged out, as if happy aliens had just taken over his body.

"What happened to you?" David asked.

"I got the sign."

David jerked his head up quickly, but he'd missed it.

"I'll see you later," Mickey said.

"Where are you going?"

"Over there," Mickey said. He began to go up her

steps. "I'll see you in school tomorrow."

"We don't go to the same school."

"Sounds good," Mickey said. The door opened and there was Philippa Frady, wearing nothing but a bathrobe.

"Hi, baby," Mickey said. "I missed you."

"You big dummy," Philippa said. "Last night my dad said if I ever see you again he's going to send me to one of those schools they have on boats in the Caribbean." And she threw her arms around him.

"Where are your parents?"

"Having dinner up at Bolo. I'm supposed to meet them there, but I think I forgot."

They moved back into Philippa's house, which rivaled the Flood house for hugeness. But because Philippa was an only child, and she wasn't allowed to have parties, the whole place was incredibly clean, almost like a museum.

"What do you want to do instead?" Mickey asked.

"I want us to be the most romantic couple in the whole world," Philippa said. "We can be like Romeo and Juliet."

They crept upstairs to her room.

"Let's just be us," Mickey said.

too little kelli, too many guys

Arno paced back and forth in Miami International Airport, waiting for Kelli. He was wearing white pajama pants, a torn black T-shirt, and no shoes, which he'd argued about with airport security twice already. But he wanted to look totally cool for Kelli, because now, for reasons he didn't quite get, he was vying for her against Randall Oddy. Arno didn't particularly like a challenge, but he definitely had one.

"What's up, lover?" Kelli came up behind him and grabbed his stomach and kissed him on the cheek. He thought she smelled like fabric softener and daisies and airline daiquiris.

"Hi," he whispered. He knew he sounded shy and wondered what was going on. Normally, if he was going to meet a girl, he liked to show up with another girl, or two other girls, so they'd be jealous of each other and subsequently make out with him quicker. But he kept forgetting about other girls when he was thinking about Kelli.

Then he noticed that Randall Oddy was with her. Arno rubbed his eyes, but Randall didn't go away.

"Hey, kid," Randall said. "I missed my plane so when I saw Kelli I jumped on her."

They laughed and bumped up against each other.

"My—" But Arno managed to catch himself before he said *dad* and added *isn't going to give you another show if you try to get with my girl.*

"Your?"

"Car is downstairs," Arno said. He'd borrowed an extremely cool 1974 white Cadillac convertible from the manager of his dad's gallery, and he had it downstairs. He could barely drive it, being from the city and all, but he'd figured on Kelli driving, which would've been really cute. But now he'd have to, as he was damned if Randall Oddy was going to sit anywhere but in the backseat.

"Your dad ready to rock tonight?" Randall asked. He threw his arm around Arno, who glared at him. Randall was wearing an Annihilate the Rich T-shirt, Prada flip-flops, and paint-splattered jeans. Arno restrained a strong inclination to point at Randall, scream *terrorist*, and run away with Kelli.

Outside it was painfully bright and blistering hot. There were palm trees everywhere and the sultry weather slowed them down as they walked to the car.

"I really like it here," Kelli said.

"I thought you would," Arno and Randall said at the same time.

During the drive, everybody sang along to the awful top 40 hit radio station, which played a lot of Latin stuff that Kelli knew better than both of them. She could really belt out a song. And so there she sat, cross-legged in the passenger seat, while Randall lounged in the back and Arno drove white-knuckled through the late-afternoon Miami traffic. They made a pretty cool-looking threesome, not that it meant much to Arno.

"La la la la la, O mi corazon!" Kelli sang out. A couple of guys in a red BMW drove up close and sang along with her.

Arno made eye contact with Randall in the rearview mirror. They glared at each other. Meanwhile, Kelli accepted a party invitation from the BMW guys.

They arrived at Arno's parents' house, a Spanish-style stucco four-story mansion right on Ocean Drive, parked, and walked around the house to the backyard, where there was a pool with fadeaway edges.

"I've got to get into that pool," Kelli said. She dropped her bags and stared.

"Me, too," Randall said.

"Guests are coming for cocktails at six," Arno said.

"They can get in, too," Randall said. He pulled off his T-shirt and jeans. Arno stared at him. Was he going to jump in naked? Arno puffed up his chest. He started to take off his clothes, too.

"Waitasecond, boys. I need my bikini," Kelli said. "There's no way I'm going skinny-dipping in the daytime."

"Aww," Randall said. He stuck out his tongue, yanked down his boxers, and jumped in the pool. Arno and Kelli stared at him. Arno could hear his parents coming through the glass doors.

Arno said, "What a hoser."

"Mmm," Kelli said. Arno had the sickening feeling that Kelli liked what she was seeing.

"Come on in! The water's excellent."

"Not till later," Kelli said. "Hi, Mr. and Mrs. Wildenburger! What a wonderful house you have."

And then, while Randall Oddy treaded water, fast, because the water was awfully clear, Arno's parents talked with Kelli. His parents seemed willing to ignore the fact that their son was in his boxers and there was a naked artist in their pool.

"Rrrr," Arno said, and put his pants back on.

david can't even make a layup

"Hey, crybaby!"

"Shut the fuck up," David said.

The Potterton basketball team was in the middle of a freshman-varsity scrimmage. David was center, slapping down balls coming from every direction, and even dunking, desperately trying to think of nothing but basketball, and then Adam Rickenbacher, this handsome freshman Jonathan didn't like for some reason, had started cracking wise.

"Sorry, dude. I know you're sensitive," Rickenbacher said.

"I'm going to kick your ass, Rickybashay," David said.

But his heart wasn't in it. He went up and ripped the ball out of Adam's hands, and Adam let him, but then some other freshman whipped around his back and whispered *Waaa*. David let another kid get the ball away from him and he walked off the court, slammed against the blue padded wall of the gym, and sat down.

"David, get back in there!" yelled Vijay Singram, the coach. He was usually a pretty mellow guy, but there were some prospective parents and their kids watching, so he was trying to look fierce. That made everything worse for David—the coach yelling, and the freshman, and a bunch of prospective eighth graders who'd probably heard he was a good player all staring at him. Before he knew it, David had jammed his shirt up into his face and started to bawl like he was six and somebody had kicked him right out of the sandbox.

"Everybody keep playing," yelled Coach Singram. He went over to David.

"Someone kill me," David said under his breath.

"What's the matter? We need you out there."

"Just a sec."

"Girl problems? Is that what it is? 'Cause that's what everybody's telling me, you know?"

"Please, could you leave me alone?" David said and peeked through his hands. He could see veins bulging in Singram's neck and sweat drip down his forehead.

"Me?" Coach Singram thundered. He looked around at the half dozen parents who were still watching him. Then the game slowly came to an end, and the freshman squad and everybody on the varsity team was watching.

"Are you going to force me to make an example

out of you?"

"Force you?" David said. "What do you mean force you? I'm not *forcing* you to do anything."

David suddenly felt too ill to speak. He stood, slowly. He sagged a little, and Adam Rickenbacher walked over and held him up by the elbow. David didn't like it, but he ended up leaning on Adam.

"Now you listen here, young man, what you do in your free time is your business, but when you bring the sad fact that your girlfriend cheated on you onto my basketball court, then it's my problem!"

"Take it easy, coach," Adam Rickenbacher said.

"What've you got to say for yourself, David?" Singram yelled.

"Thanks for the pep talk."

"Get out of here!"

"I'm already gone," David said. He pushed Adam away and slumped off toward the showers, with nothing but the sound of laughter and bouncing balls behind him.

another oddy opening for arno

"My parents' house is so big," Arno said to Kelli. "We can stay in a guest wing and they won't even know we're there."

"That's nice," Kelli said. "I just met the most amazing woman—she owns this nightclub in South Beach that's not even open yet. Her name is Ingrid Casares and she says I should come by there later and we can dance and she'll serve us drinks. But that's not for a few more hours. What do you want to do now?"

"Don't worry," Arno said. "I'll think of something."

He stood with her outside his parents' gallery on Lincoln Road. Even though the opening was officially over, there were still tons of people inside, all loving Randall Oddy's work. This had been a good thing for Arno, because Randall had been more or less dragged away from Kelli by a bunch of collectors. Meanwhile, Arno had slowly made it out of the gallery with Kelli without anyone calling after them.

"We could go back inside and look for Randall,"

Kelli said.

"Yeah, but is that the most fun thing you can think of?"

"No," Kelli said, and smiled.

Just then a valet showed up in front of them with the white Cadillac. Arno hadn't called for it. But here it was, and it had the keys in it.

"Thanks," Arno said to the valet, and hopped in. He beckoned to Kelli, who shrugged and got in the passenger side.

"Let's drive back to the house," Arno said.

"Wait!" someone behind them screamed. Arno saw the gallery manager who owned the Cadillac screaming and waving, but he just turned up the radio.

At a stoplight, Arno turned to Kelli. She was smiling, so he kissed her, first on the neck and then on the lips. Her skin was hot from a day in the sun, and she laughed a little and kissed him back. *Finally*, Arno thought. This was by far the most work he'd ever done for a girl. A driver behind him honked his horn.

A few minutes later they pulled into the white pebble drive at his house. It was quiet there, and he took Kelli's hand and led her around the side of the house, to the pool.

"Let's go for that swim now," he said.

Kelli didn't speak. They crept around the corner and

there were candles set out near the swimming pool. A bottle of champagne was in an ice bucket that was bobbing up and down in the middle of a life preserver. Music played, a light samba rhythm. Arno sniffed the air: incense. He hadn't planned any of this. He was instantly furious, and wondered if Randall had somehow gotten out of the opening and arrived before them. Where the hell was he? Arno gripped Kelli's hand tighter, and looked around him. How had Randall moved so fast?

"Oh my God," Kelli said.

That's when Arno saw his parents come through the glass doors wearing nothing but towels. Like him and Kelli, they were holding hands.

"Oh no," Arno said. The towels dropped. His parents were making out. They were naked.

He felt Kelli wrestle her hand away from his.

"Gross," she whispered. Arno's parents started to kiss more intensely. Kelli and Arno watched, momentarily stunned, like witnesses to a car crash.

"Too gross!" Kelli said, and quickly ran back to the car.

"No, Kelli, wait—" Arno said. He ran after her. He'd never been so confused in his life.

"Please take me back to the gallery," Kelli said. She sat in the passenger seat, with both her hands over her eyes.

Arno pulled the big white car out of the driveway as quietly as possible, and he didn't open his mouth, or look at Kelli, who was loudly chewing what looked like Blue Blowout Bubblicious and examining her nails. Arno drove slowly and did everything he could to delete from his brain the image of his parents embracing naked by candlelight in front of the family pool.

mickey blows it big time

On Wednesday morning, Mickey Pardo decided to go to school. He'd convinced himself that he was finally coming down from his painkiller cloud, and anyway he'd been sort of missing the place. So he showed up for second-period physics class and really enjoyed listening to Mrs. Alsadir go on about a load of trippy shit involving quarks. He couldn't follow much of it, but it was all kind of cool anyway.

"Are there any questions?" Mrs. Alsadir asked.

"I just want to say I am totally loving this trippy shit!" Mickey called out.

Mrs. Alsadir just smiled uncomfortably and went on with the lesson. Mickey didn't have a textbook or a notebook or a pen. He sat in the back row, alone. And after a while he climbed up on the lab station in front of him and lay on his side. Still Mrs. Alsadir said nothing.

Then he got a call from Jonathan, so he decided to take it, and shuffled out into the hall. He was wearing a brown jumpsuit, his combat boots, and he had some old necklaces strewn around his neck, along with a pair of black aviator glasses. His cast was huge and gleaming and white, except for the places where he'd spilled coffee and food on it.

"Will you be returning?" Mrs. Alsadir called out. He ignored her.

"Dude?" Mickey said to the phone.

"Anything interesting happening?" Jonathan asked. "I've been looking for Arno—he should be back. Can you believe he went down to Florida with my cousin?"

"Huh," Mickey said. He smelled something good, like bacon, and looked around.

"She had a day between her NYU interview and her Sarah Lawrence interview, so she went down to South Beach. I don't even want to think about what they did down there. And I had to cover for her, and now she's back. But Arno didn't come in today. Have you seen David?"

"He goes to Potterton, remember?" Mickey said. "I'm at Talbot."

"Oh yeah. Listen, I'll check you later."

"Sounds good." Mickey looked up and down the corridor. What was that good smell? A small eighth grader came down the corridor then, and he was eating something. A BLT. Mickey looked at it. Mmm.

"Mickey Pardo," a stern male voice said. But Mickey didn't hear. He dropped the phone. The kid with the BLT kept coming.

"Actually, why don't I come by your house after school," Jonathan said, to air. "We'll go find Arno together."

Mickey spread his arms wide, like he was signaling that he was about to make a fair catch. He wanted that sandwich. The eighth grader tried to pass him on the left, then on the right.

"Mickey Pardo!" the adult male voice yelled. Too late. Mickey had wrapped the kid up in his cast and the sandwich was up in the air.

"Wait," the kid said, his voice muffled by the fact that his head was jammed into Mickey's chest.

Mickey pushed the sandwich toward his mouth and heard voices all around him. He felt like he hadn't eaten in days. As he closed his jaw, the sandwich shot into the air and Mickey closed his mouth on something soft that was still moving. *Mmm, bacon*, Mickey thought.

"Aaah!" the eighth grader screamed, as Mickey bit into his hand.

And then Mickey was slowly separated from his food. And phone calls were made. And he was being sent home for biting an eighth grader.

david connects some of the dots

"Have you seen Patch?" Jonathan asked. He and David were standing in front of Mickey's parents' building, waiting for somebody to let them in.

"Not since I can remember," David said. "I keep meaning to call, but I'm too upset to find him."

"I guess that means you haven't seen Amanda?"

"Not since I broke up with her," David said slowly. He still couldn't believe he'd done it, and he still had no idea who she'd cheated on him with—but that was okay, he knew he couldn't have dealt with it if he had known.

"Oh, right," Jonathan said.

"And I started crying again yesterday, during basketball practice. I may have to quit the team out of complete humiliation."

"Really?"

"It was awful. Now everybody is calling me the Most Sensitive Guy in the World. And if it hadn't been for that Adam kid, I might've taken a swing at my coach."

"Oh yeah, that kid's lame," Jonathan said.

"He's okay with me," David said. "Anyway, I don't know what I'm going to do, because the team is my whole identity besides Amanda. I walk by mirrors now and I can't see my own reflection."

"You're like a Lifetime movie," Jonathan said. "You know that?"

"I'm depressed."

"We'll work on you this weekend. I got some ideas."

The door opened and they looked at Ricardo Pardo's head assistant, Caselli. He wore a white jumpsuit and had a shaved head. Tattoos were visible on his neck and wrists. David could never figure out why all of Ricardo Pardo's assistants were so tough.

Caselli said, "You guys can't come in. Mickey's in big trouble."

"What'd he do?" Jonathan asked, and sighed.

"Apparently he tried to eat a kid at school."

"Did he break the skin?" Jonathan asked. "He's done this before and he won't get expelled if he didn't break the skin."

"Can we just see him for five minutes?" David asked. "We need to check in with him about homework."

"Except you don't go to his school," Caselli said. "But whatever. Don't let his dad see you."

Jonathan and David crept quietly inside. The house was cavernous, with twenty-foot-high ceilings and enormous doors leading from room to room. Opera, *L'Elisir D'Amore*, blasted through all the speakers on the first floor. As they passed the studio, they could see Ricardo Pardo and about five helpers making huge art out of mangled car parts.

They found Mickey in his room, lying on the cold concrete floor where his bed should have been.

"Where's your bed?" Jonathan asked.

"I don't know," Mickey said. "What does it matter? Now I'm in trouble and I can't see Philippa again."

"You should've never gotten off the phone with me."

"Yeah, Jonathan. That's what it was." Mickey sat up and looked at his friends. "Jonathan, I didn't know you had to wear a blazer to school."

"We don't," Jonathan said. He tugged at the sleeves of his brown tweed blazer.

"Then why are you wearing one now?"

"I felt kind of serious today," Jonathan said. "Unlike you."

"You felt serious, so you dressed up like a science teacher," Mickey said. David and Mickey shook their heads.

"Yeah," Jonathan said. "And you think you're a spaceman, so you always wear a jumpsuit."

"You tried to eat a kid?" David asked. He sat down in a windowsill, next to a pile of schoolbooks and a Macintosh notebook that was unplugged and covered in dust. The roomed smelled faintly of paint.

"I thought he had a BLT in his hand."

"Did he?" David asked.

"No, it was a copy of *The Sun Also Rises*. But it looked and smelled like a BLT."

"If it was the paperback, I can imagine it," Jonathan said. "So you bit him."

"Yeah." Mickey got up off the floor. He went over to his stereo and put on some Slayer. The music was pretty loud and David didn't feel like it was doing much to make any of them feel better.

"Look, has Arno been in touch with you?"

"No," Mickey said. "But I heard from some kid in school that he took your cousin down to Florida and had an orgy with her. Man, that girl is impressive. I'm just glad I love my girlfriend because otherwise I'd hit on Kelli and that'd be no good."

"What's so no-good about her?" Jonathan asked.

"I can't believe you're defending her," David said suddenly. He looked quickly at Mickey and then Jonathan. "You introduce her to us, and next thing I know, Amanda cheats on me and Mickey falls off a building."

"That happens every weekend," Jonathan said.

"Not really it doesn't. I wouldn't be surprised if Amanda cheated with Kelli. That girl is bad luck." David pulled his hood over his head.

"Oh come on, she's my cousin."

"Liza thinks she's a bitch, too," David said. "Jane told me."

"You two are assholes," Jonathan said. He stood up. So did Mickey. Then Mickey thumped Jonathan once on the chest with his cast and Jonathan fell on the floor with a thud.

"Ow! What the hell'd you do that for?"

"We're trying to talk some sense into you," Mickey said. "Your cousin is a demon from hell."

"She's from St. Louis. And she may not be the classiest girl in the world, but she's not a demon." Jonathan stood up and dusted himself off.

"Although," Jonathan added, "if she were as bad as everyone says, it'd explain why she's so into Arno."

"Even Arno is better than she is," David said. "I mean, I trust him more."

Jonathan stared at David and said, "I think I'd better go. I've got to go home and read the screenplay of *Donnie Darko* for English."

"Should I not be trusting Arno?" David asked. He reached behind him, found that he was close enough to the wall, and leaned against it. A queasy feeling had come over him. "You stay here," David said. "I'm the one who should go."

David walked out of Mickey's room and down the long corridor toward the front door. On the way he passed Ricardo Pardo, who was puffing on a cigar the size of a hot dog and singing almost as loudly as the opera was playing.

"Hey!" Ricardo yelled at David. "You're not supposed to be here."

"That's why I'm leaving!" David yelled back and pulled away from Ricardo. He felt a sudden chill. Ricardo Pardo was tough and he couldn't believe he'd yelled at him.

"*Condena'o*," Ricardo said, *wiseass*, and puffed out his cheeks so his beard stood on end.

The corridor was awfully cold. Ricardo made David wait a very long and uncomfortable minute for Caselli to come and unbolt the front door, run the security code, and let him out onto West Street.

i take a walk with my little friend

Flan Flood looked concerned. "I'm getting worried about Patch."

We were holding hands and walking up Fifth Avenue. She'd said her hands were cold, and when I took one, it was. It was Thursday afternoon and I'd spent one very dull school day text-messaging people and having those messages go unanswered. Arno was back from Florida, I knew, but only because I'd heard from my mom that Kelli had had a really good interview at Sarah Lawrence earlier in the day.

"What?" I asked. I wanted to pay attention to Flan, I really did, but it was hard to do because I was so worried about my friends.

"Patch!" Flan said, and punched me in the shoulder.

"Okay, okay," I said. "Right. I haven't had a chance to think about him. Where is he?"

"I don't know and I'm getting sick of covering for him."

"When was the last time you saw your parents?"

"I don't know that either."

Flan blubbered a little. She was only about an inch shorter than me, but she seemed very small just then. I looked both ways and put my arm around her. The sun was really bright, but it was a little cold. I had on a new Andre Longacre zip-up cashmere sweater and Flan was wearing what was probably her father's button-down and jeans and red Sigerson Morrison high heels and white socks.

"Your sweater feels good," Flan said. So of course I took it off and gave it to her.

"Who's been taking care of you?"

"February," she said. She wrapped herself up in my sweater. I only had on a black T-shirt and black jeans, but that was cool.

"Seriously?"

We began to walk in the direction of the Flood house.

"Well, Patch said he'd be around, and it was just supposed to be for a couple of days at the end of last week, but then my mother went down to St. Lucia and my dad stayed up in Connecticut in that tower of his where nobody is allowed to go, and Patch was gone that whole time, so I guess I've been taking care of myself. I order sushi or Thai food sometimes for me and February, when she remembers she's hungry."

"Wait . . . Patch has been gone since last week?"

"Last Wednesday."

"Wow," I said. "And meanwhile, everybody else is in trouble, too."

"What do you mean?"

"Arno's chasing after my cousin and making an ass of himself, Mickey got suspended and maybe kicked out of school, and David broke up with his girlfriend and can't stop crying in public."

"And Patch is gone."

"Right," I said. "That, too."

We walked quietly for a little while, and then we were in front of her house. I took a quick look up and down the street. I still had my arm around her.

"Do you want to come upstairs and watch *School of Rock* on the big TV in my parents' bedroom?"

I took a deep breath. I knew what would happen if I did that and though I'm not a big fan of fighting with my own impulses, I knew I had to this time.

"I always fall asleep during that movie," I said, and moved away from her. But we were still holding hands.

"Well, we could . . . nap together."

"No. I think I shouldn't."

"Jonathan, I can't wait for you much longer."

"You shouldn't. What I said the other day—it's true. I just like hanging out with you in a friendly way. That's all."

"But then that night, you called."

"Yeah. I know those two things are totally contradictory, but still," I said. And I knew that sounded pretty lame. I was still holding her hand and I let it go. Because she was totally too young and everybody was laughing at me about hanging out with her, and stupid as it may sound, I knew that just because I was feeling something, it didn't mean it was the right thing to feel.

"Look, I'll call you later and we can figure out what to do about Patch."

"Whatever," Flan said. She was all frustrated-looking, suddenly, and she opened the door

and went into her house without saying good-
bye to me.

I wandered home. I thought I'd see how my
mom was doing. We hadn't talked in a couple of
days. But when I got in, she wasn't around. Kelli
was in my room, lying on my bed, actually.

"You're still here?" I asked.

"Yeah, we're not going back till Sunday morning. Or I might just take a different plane back
than my mom. I haven't figured it out yet. I've got
a lot of stuff to take care of here in the city."

"Um," I said. I dropped into my desk chair.
"Don't you have to go to school?"

"The stuff I'm doing here seems more
important."

"I don't get it. Your interviews are over. What
are you still doing here?"

Just then her cell phone rang. She stood up
and smiled at me like I was nine years old and it
was time for me to go to bed.

"Isn't it obvious? I'm having a really, really
good time." Then she went out of the room and I
sat for a moment, spinning the disc on my iPod,
and thinking about how I never remembered to
use it. That reminded me of the thing I needed to
do. Find Patch.

I went ahead and called Flan, and we agreed that my guys and I should meet at the Flood house the next night and find him, if he hadn't come home by then. February Flood might help, too, though Flan hadn't seen her big sister since the day before. Her mom had called from St. Lucia, so she knew her parents would be back by Sunday. Which meant we needed to find Patch before then.

I slipped on my headset, concentrated on Patch for the first time in a while, and started to speed dial the necessary people.

Mickey and Philippa were in her third-floor bedroom after school on Friday, though only Philippa had actually gone to school. They were in the middle of her bed and they were French-kissing so heavily that they kept running out of breath. Philippa had a grandfather clock in one corner that was ticking loudly, and they were listening to pre-fuse 73, because Philippa used to date a deejay and had developed a taste for arcane house music.

"I need to get over to the Floods," Mickey said as he slowly pulled away from Philippa. "I promised Jonathan."

"Come on," Philippa said. "Forget him, can't you?" She was wearing nothing except the red lingerie she'd bought at Le Petit Coquette on the way home from school. Mickey had to look away from her and close his eyes in order to form a sentence.

"Well, Patch has been missing for a while, and Jonathan needs us to help find him."

"But what about us?" Philippa said, and laughed.

"The other thing I need to do is sneak out of here before your parents come."

"That's true," Philippa said. "So you think you're really kicked out of school?"

"Actually, I think my dad is supposed to talk with your dad about that," Mickey said. He faced the wall, where there was a big painting by Randall Oddy; a beautiful green eye scrunched up and winking. Mickey stared at it. He thought it was pretty cool.

"Since my dad's on the board at Talbot."

"Right," Mickey said.

Philippa was supposed to go with her parents to their place in Amagansett in an hour, which was part of the deal she'd made with them after getting in trouble last weekend—that she'd spend more time with them and treat them like human beings and not ATM machines.

"Let's get you out of here," Philippa said.

"Come over later," Mickey said. He got up and pulled on his jumpsuit, and looked around on the floor for his boots.

"I can't. Mickey, have you completely given up on underwear? Anyway, you know I'm going away." He turned back around, and they fell onto the bed, and began to kiss again. But Mickey's phone was ringing, and they both knew who it was.

"I've got to go."

"Maybe I'll come back on the Jitney and find you tomorrow night. My parents will be sick of me by then."

"Sounds good. We'll find Patch. And then you and I can hang out. And put in a good word for me with your parents, would you?"

"Maybe that's not such a hot idea," Philippa said. Mickey nodded, because she was right.

Then he ran down the stairs as fast as he could. He had to get out of there before the Fradys came home. He was now completely forbidden to go anywhere near their daughter. He got to the front door and tried the lock, but for some reason, it didn't give. He pushed, and it seemed to pull. Then it moved on its own. *A ghost?* Mickey reared back as Jackson Frady pulled open the door.

"Ah, Mr. Pardo," Mr. Frady said. "What a pleasant surprise."

"Uh, I was just going to leave, actually."

"No, Mr. Pardo, your plans have been changed. The six of us will dine tonight."

"Six?"

"Our daughter, your parents, and of course my wife and I. And you. Six."

Mickey looked around. He pointed at his chest. Me? Six? Shit.

"We'll take this opportunity to straighten a few things out once and for all."

arno can't connect his emotions and his actions

Before going out, Arno put on a black suit even though he normally never wore that sort of thing. He thought it would make him feel better. It was a Ralph Lauren purple label suit and he was basically stealing it from his father, who was still down in Florida. Arno was in his room, getting ready to go over to the Flood house. He played Bright Eyes and sang along. It wasn't that he liked Kelli. It was just that she kept saying no. And that was making him feel extremely weird.

"Which one of us would be the foolish one?" he sang out. "Which one of us'd be the fool? Could you please start explaining? You know I need some understanding!"

And then he threw himself on his bed, bawling, without having a clue why.

Then the phone rang. Jonathan.

"Where the hell are you, dude?"

"I'm coming. I'm just . . ." But he couldn't even think of the word. After he got off the phone, he just stood there in his dad's suit and a ripped white Oxford shirt, and he wished he had someone to talk to. Finally he had the idea to call Liza Komansky. She'd always been nice to him. She would understand.

"Aren't you over at the Floods? Finding Patch?" Liza asked.

"Yeah," he said. "I'm on my way there. I'm on the street, but I was thinking it'd be great to see you first."

"Well you'll probably see me later," she said, "when the whole thing turns into a party."

"But I need to see you now."

"Why?"

"I just do."

"Well," she said. "Okay."

They made a plan to meet for a very quick burger at the Corner Bistro, where Arno never got carded.

Arno grabbed a booth in the back where you could practically set off M-80s and no one would notice. Liza came in a few minutes later. It had started to rain. Liza's black hair was dewy and wet and when she sat down, she tried to lick a drop of water off the tip of her nose and Arno reached out and flicked it out of the way. Then they looked at each other. Liza pulled back to the wall and smiled at Arno.

"Thanks for seeing me."

"No problem," Liza said.

160

They ordered burgers and some two-dollar Rheingold, which tasted like colored soda water.

"It's just—" Arno said. But then he couldn't say it. How could he? He was Arno. So he sulked, and he pouted, and he was weirdly unable to do anything but scratch his black crocodile loafer, which was nowhere near as bizarre as what Jonathan wore on his feet. Finally, Liza came over to his side of the bench.

"Do you want me to say it?" Liza asked.

Arno was literally pouting. He was thinking about Kelli, the lopsided grin, the white-blond hair and the dark eyebrows, the way she looked like she was naked and daydreaming about sex even when she was dressed and probably thinking about the next important New York person she could make like her. And now she was somewhere with Randall Oddy and who knew who else, doing some underhanded art stuff, or worse, posing for him or something. *Man.*

"Do you know that story about Courtney Love?" Arno asked. "How when she was fifteen she made a list of what she wanted to do and number three after make a hit record and be an actor in Hollywood was 'Make friends with Michael Stipe'?"

"Yeah," Liza said. "That kind of climbing is gross. But you're off the subject."

"What subject?" Arno asked.

"The thing that you want me to say."

"Oh, right," Arno said miserably. "Say it."

"You've always been really attracted to me and you didn't want to say anything because of Jonathan."

"Um."

Liza rubbed Arno's cheek with the back of her hand. She sipped her beer. Their burgers arrived and were placed on the other side of the table. And they both knew that if they didn't eat them in the next five minutes, they'd shrivel and taste like cold rocks.

"But the thing is, Arno, I'm done with Jonathan. I can't wait for him anymore, and who knows what he's up to with Patch's little sister, which is completely batty and disturbing, and anyway . . . I think about you, too."

"You do?" Arno looked at his food. He knew he wouldn't get a chance to eat it. Why hadn't he just fooled around with Kelli right when he met her? Then he could forget about her now.

"Yeah," Liza said. "A lot."

So Arno leaned over and kissed her, before she said more embarrassing stuff. They ended up making out for ten minutes, then twenty. Liza was pretty hot in an extremely understated way and it was kind of true, he'd always thought she was supposed to be with Jonathan. But it wasn't like he wanted this. In fact, he didn't.

162

"I need to go," Arno said.

"Let's not tell anybody about this."

"That's a really good idea."

"Not till we're ready."

"I'm with you on that," Arno said. "Let's keep it a secret for a long time."

And after they'd kissed good-bye and he took off down the block, his head went back to the same place it had been since last Friday night, right after he'd stopped fooling around with Amanda and had seen Kelli. Kelli. He wished she'd leave so he could forget her. And what about David? Did David know that he had fooled around with Amanda? Would Amanda have said something? He hoped not. Arno shrugged to himself.

When it came to all this emotional stuff and not hurting people, he really didn't have a clue.

welcome back to friday night

i never asked to be the referee

During the afternoon, I bought a new pair of shoes. I don't want to call this a Friday ritual. It's not that at all. It's just that every once in a while, and usually it's on Fridays, I head up to Madison Avenue and buy a new pair of loafers. Today it was a black leather pair with ridged rubber bottoms from Prada and they were pretty hot. They looked like little Porsche Carreras or something, so I went sockless, with some old khakis and a black hooded Penguin sweatshirt over a black polo. I blew two hours before I got myself over to the Flood house, because I had to stop at home and ditch the shoe box, since I didn't want to show up with some extra shoes and have to change—I'd never hear the end of it if I did that.

When I got up the stairs and rang the bell, I felt nervous about David and Arno seeing each other, and knowing that I hadn't handled Flan well wasn't helping either. At least she wasn't supposed to be around. She was going to the movies and then staying at Dylan's house. And I hoped she wasn't just doing that on account of me being around.

The door opened. David stared at me.

"Everybody here?" I asked.

"Just me and Arno."

"Oh," I said quietly. I figured Arno hadn't told David anything, because David looked sad and normal, not angry.

We went into the living room, which one of the maids had rearranged after last weekend's blowout. It looked very clean, and Arno was sitting on the couch with his legs crossed, in one of his father's five-thousand-dollar suits, with a bottle of Grolsch sweating on his knee.

"You look sallow," I said and sat on a chair between Arno, who hadn't gotten up, and David, who'd taken the couch across from him.

"What's that mean?"

"Pale. Limp. Colorless. Shouldn't you have gotten tan in Florida? How many days of school did you miss?"

"I went in for a while on Thursday," Arno said. He sounded totally down and David looked unhappy, too. But I didn't think either of them knew *why* they were feeling like that. And I didn't want to say if they didn't already know.

"I heard they're still calling you the Most Sensitive Guy in the World," I said to David.

"Yeah. But that kid Adam Rickenbacher is trying to keep people from saying it so much. Maybe it was him that Amanda made out with and that's why he's acting so nice."

"I doubt that," I said, and glared at Arno, who was staring at the floor.

Then none of us said anything for a little while. But we were all, I'm sure, mostly thinking that it'd be great if Mickey would show up and fling something that belonged to the Floods against the wall, and then these two could just have it out, discover who did what to whom, and get it over with, so we could all be friends again.

My phone rang and it was Mickey.

"I'm at a dinner," he said. "Start without me."

"We can't start without you."

"Can't be there till ten."

"*Where* are you?"

"I've landed in hell," he said, and clicked off.

Mickey, his parents, Philippa, and her parents were in La Palme D'Or, an old restaurant in a house on Charles Street. The place was made up to look like the late 1800s, so everything was lit with candles, all the surfaces were mahogany, and the wallpaper was painted with a thicket of pink flowers. A waiter in a nineteenth-century livery costume delivered their appetizers while everyone watched in silence.

"Now before we get into the trouble we're having with you at home, what about this little trouble at school?" Mr. Frady began as he dug into a steaming plate of snails.

"I'll do whatever you say to make things better, Mr. Frady," Mickey said. He eyed Philippa, who sat next to him.

"Of course a written apology and community service would be only a beginning," Mr. Frady said. He was a very tall man with bushy eyebrows, a lot of nose and ear hair, and his own investment banking company. He always stared Mickey right in the eyes, and Mickey hated him for it. But Mickey knew that without Mr. Frady, he'd be kicked out of school for good. He felt his phone vibrate in his pocket, but he didn't pick it up. He sighed.

"I agree," he said. He felt Philippa's hand on his thigh and squeezed it. A waiter came to the table and poured wine for the parents and Philippa. He stopped at Mickey's glass, but all four parents waved the waiter away.

Mickey picked at a salad of shredded bits of duck and cabbage that he didn't recall ordering. His silver fork was heavy in his hand and he felt himself sinking into his heavily embroidered chair. A fire burned merrily in a fireplace behind him and Mickey considered chucking himself into it. That or ease a log out onto the rug, wait for it to smolder, scream *fire,* and run the hell out of the place.

Jackson Frady nodded at Mickey and began to speak to Ricardo Pardo, who was on his right. Mickey's father was pushed back so there was room for his belly to breathe, and he was stroking his beard and glaring at everyone. Mickey's mother sat next to him, looking shockingly beautiful in a black dress and plenty of gold jewelry. They were both watching Mickey. Things were bad. Mickey sighed.

"*Hijo de la chingada*," Mickey whispered. *Son of a bitch.*

"*Haz el favor de comportarte!*" Lucy Pardo said. *Try to behave!*

"*Lo siento, Mamá*," Mickey said. *I'm sorry, Mom.*

The waiter came back and poured Mickey some water.

"Could I get a Jack Daniels on the rocks?" Mickey asked the waiter.

"Are you kidding?" Ricardo Pardo asked. He was halfway through his second double Absolut Limon, one ice cube.

"Um, yes," Mickey said. "I totally was." He sank lower in his chair. He had to rest his cast on the table, where it lay, messy and brown, a cold reminder of why he was in trouble and how, come Monday, he was probably going to get kicked out of school for good, unless Jackson Frady decided to help him out.

"About that problem Mickey's having at school," Mr. Frady said to Ricardo.

"Can you fix it?" Ricardo asked.

"I don't see why not," Mr. Frady said. "After all, I'm on the board. There's just one thing."

"What?" Ricardo asked. "About these two—they can never see each other again!"

"I agree with you on that. But I was thinking about

our garden in Amagansett. It seems so spare lately."

Mickey shook his head. He'd seen their garden. It was the size of a couple of football fields and it was right on the water. Normal people would've called it a park next to a beach.

"You want a sculpture?" Ricardo asked. "Is that what you're asking for?"

"Well, now that you mention it," Mr. Frady said. And the two men put their heads together, and began to strike a deal. Ricardo glared at his son the whole time.

Meanwhile, the two women went back to gossiping about Arno's parents, about how they were seeing a therapist in order to put the spice back in their marriage and the therapist was making them do outrageous stuff, like get caught having sex in front of their maids down in Florida. It was disgusting!

"But maybe it could be fun," Mrs. Frady said, and giggled. Mrs. Pardo rolled her eyes.

Of course, the therapist was Sam Grobart, David's dad. But nobody said that aloud, not in front of Mickey and Philippa, who knew it perfectly well and didn't care.

"I think I need to go to a party now," Mickey said.

"*Tienes que esperar a tu papá,*" Lucy Pardo said. *You have to wait for your dad.* "Then you can go have your party."

"Yes, Mama." Mickey sighed.

"Of course," Jackson Frady said, "after we resolve this problem at school, we need to discuss just what to do with this boy and our home. He keeps breaking in. We don't like that."

"He breaks in?" Ricardo Pardo asked. He turned to his son. *"Mira que te va a salir caro!"* *You're going to pay for this!*

"But, Papa!" Mickey argued.

"Cálmate, loco," Ricardo said. *Cool it, crazy.*

"Looks like we'll be here for a while," Jackson Frady said. He smiled and took a sip of his wine.

the search party skids onto arno's thin ice

"We were in love," David said. He was on his third bottle of beer. He and Arno and Jonathan were still waiting for Mickey and not telling each other the truth about anything.

"If that's true, then you'll get back together," Arno said. He kept looking at Jonathan as if to say *help me*, but Jonathan didn't seem to want to.

"But she doesn't want to!"

"If she doesn't want to—" Jonathan cut Arno off. "This was supposed to be about Patch." He had his arms folded. The three of them had gone down to the breakfast area in the Flood kitchen, where they were huddled around take-out Thai food—tom yum soup, spring rolls, roast pork pad Thai, and a lot of Tsingha beer. February Flood had come home with some people and taken over the parlor floor, where they were drinking flaming shots of Bacardi 151.

Arno's phone rang. He took the call, smiled, and began to whisper into it.

David's head was starting to hang down. He pulled his bowl of soup toward him and began to slurp it.

"You are the most miserable person to be miserable around," Jonathan said. "I mean, you really wallow. At college you'll end up living in a single with no friends but the hall adviser. I'm trying to help you, but man, where's your balls?"

"I thought we were friends," David said, and slumped lower.

"She's coming over!" Arno said.

He actually got up from the table and danced. Someone who had come down on a beer run snickered and Arno whipped around.

"Get lost, you little fucker!"

Everyone looked and the snickerer was Adam Rickenbacher.

"Leave him alone," David said. He nodded an okay to the freshman.

"I wonder what he's doing here," Jonathan said.

"Kelli's bringing Randall Oddy, but she's still coming."

"We may leave before then," Jonathan said. "We need to go look for Patch."

"Look for him where?" Arno said. "He'll turn up. He probably got some really good ice cream and stayed in the store. He probably fell in love with an ice cream

175

flavor and went somewhere to live with it."

"The Floods are coming back on Sunday. If we don't find him by tomorrow night, we should go to the police."

"Oh yeah," Arno said, and hoisted his beer. "That's a great idea."

"Well—" Jonathan said.

Arno did a little shimmy. Kelli was coming! He'd already asked to visit her in St. Louis. He'd bought all of Nelly's albums and found Missouri on the map. Who cared if he kept fooling around with other girls? When he closed his eyes, he felt her makeup against his cheek, her soft body against his hard chest. . . . She was definitely into him. It had to be.

"Arno!"

"What?"

"Stick with us. As soon as we find Patch, you can get back to fantasizing about Kelli."

"But we haven't even figured out who—" David stopped talking and looked up the stairs. "I need to go talk to that Rickenbacher kid. If he's being cool because he got with Amanda . . ." He stood up and went after him.

"The only thing that kid ever gave it to is his pillow," Jonathan said. He stood up and looked at Arno. "Now when are you going to tell David the truth?"

"Do I have to?" Arno asked.

"Kind of. Unless you want your whole life to be a lie."

The kitchen was pretty quiet now, except for the rumbles coming through the ceiling from upstairs. Arno thought about David. He didn't mean him any harm. He'd spilled some soup on his suit pants and he slapped at the stain. He thought about how upset he'd be at Randall Oddy if he'd made out with Kelli.

"I'll tell him later," Arno said. "I just hope Amanda gets back together with him. I sure don't want her."

"That's nice of you to say," Jonathan said.

"Look, I promise I'll never touch Liza again. I mean Amanda."

"I just want us to be friends once this is all over. That's all I care about," Jonathan said.

"That's nice of you to say," Arno said. And then they were both quiet as they listened to David come back downstairs.

"Was it him?" Arno asked, with a trace of hope in his voice.

"No," David said. "That was ridiculous of me." He got another beer.

"Then what's he doing here, anyway?" Jonathan asked. Arno watched, but for reasons he couldn't follow, David wouldn't say anything, or meet Jonathan's eyes.

Arno checked his watch. It was already past eleven. Jonathan went upstairs to see who else was around.

"I guess he's got his own girl problems," David said. "He's not into Amanda, that's for sure."

Then they heard the front door bang open above their heads, and there was a kind of crying out that was similar to the noise an unhappy tiger makes, and they knew Mickey had arrived.

mickey makes it out alive

"That dinner was hell," Mickey said. "Philippa's dad tried to blackmail my dad out of a million dollars in art, all to get me out of trouble. They got in this huge argument about it and me and Philippa went to the bathroom together and then we were like, let's just duck out. So we're here. Where's beer?" he asked. But there was none in the fridge. He looked over at David and Arno, who were still sitting at the kitchen table. He grabbed David's beer and gulped it down.

"That's better," Mickey said. "Philippa's upstairs with Liza and a bunch of other people. And they're even starting to get worried about Patch." Mickey stared at David and Arno. "What's the matter with you two?" Mickey couldn't figure out the deal with David and Arno. They looked sad about girls, but Mickey knew they couldn't possibly be sad for the same kinds of reasons.

"Those girls love Patch," David said.

"Because he's nice to them," Arno added.

"And he's funny."

"He doesn't try anything with them but he's really good-looking, in a dope-smoker kind of way."

"When you two get done with your pity party, let me know," Mickey said. "I'm going upstairs to see who wants to get wasted."

Mickey turned around and walked out of the kitchen, leaving David and Arno alone. He thought they were the weirdest pair: the black-haired smoothie in the suit and the most sensitive basketball player in the world.

On the way upstairs, Mickey grabbed a bottle of Heineken from some kid.

"Hey!" Adam Rickenbacher said.

"You shouldn't be drinking anyway," Mickey said.

"You're right," Adam said. "I have better things to do." And he scooted out of Mickey's reach and up the stairs. Mickey walked by Amanda and Philippa and Liza, who were whispering, their heads nearly touching. He tried to butt in, but Philippa pushed him away with her elbow.

"Not now," she whispered.

Just then the door opened and Jonathan's cousin walked in with some artist Mickey vaguely recognized and some other adults who were dressed like kids. He was pretty sure they were adults, anyway.

"Hi, Mickey!" Kelli called out.

"Hey, Ooh," Mickey said.

She came running over and gave him a kiss. She was dressed in a black miniskirt and a black T-shirt that said *I'm the Talent.*

"Arno's downstairs," he said. "That dude's in love with you."

"He doesn't even know what love is," Kelli said. Mickey raised an eyebrow. She had a point. The artist put a possessive hand on Kelli, who didn't seem to notice.

"I think I know you," Mickey said to Randall. "And I'm pretty sure my dad says your art sucks."

"Who's your dad?" Randall looked like he was about to laugh.

Mickey looked back at Amanda and Philippa and Liza. They were really glaring. Not at him, he figured. Not at the artist guy. Kelli. They hated Kelli. That figured. She was pretty hot.

"My dad is Ricardo Pardo," Mickey said. The guy paled. Suddenly his face was the color of his white leather jacket.

"Oh shit," Randall said.

Mickey laughed. He didn't like arrogant young art guys any more than the next high schooler. Especially not when they were hanging out with seventeen-year-old girls from St. Louis.

"When's she leaving?" he heard Amanda whisper,

loud. She was always the loudest of her group.

"What do you care?" Kelli said, and squared off against Amanda. Then Amanda got right up in Kelli's face.

"You're screwing everything up," Amanda said. "You're just lucky you didn't get with the guy I like."

"Oh, come on," Kelli said. "What could you even do to stop me?"

"Oh my God," Amanda said, laughing. "As if I can't scheme with the best of them?" She turned back to Liza and Philippa, but they weren't behind her anymore. Mickey had finished his beer and found another one, where someone had left it on the mantelpiece. The room had slowly begun to fill with kids everyone knew but no one knew that well, and the music had switched to some haunting Belle and Sebastian.

Mickey looked around. He smelled nothing but beer, and he could feel Kelli's artist and his friends whispering about him. He played with his goggles and wondered for the second time that week where his Vespa had gone. Meanwhile, Kelli was still in front of him.

"You know what?" Mickey said. "I'm going to go get Arno. Maybe he can help straighten all this out."

Mickey whipped around to get downstairs and find Arno, but when he looked, he saw that Arno was already headed their way.

arno takes hits from all directions

"Kelli?" Arno called out. He had stopped a couple of steps before the landing, so he was cut off at the chest. Clearly he didn't know he looked like a midget, but he felt like one.

"Kelli?" he said again. He looked around, but the big room was dark and the music was loud. And it was Liza who came up to him. She was definitely high on the list of people he didn't want to see just then.

"Do you want to go up to the roof?" Liza asked. He wondered why she hadn't heard which name he'd called. The relevant people—Kelli, Mickey, Amanda—all went still for a moment. And then David walked up the stairs and stood there, watching.

"Liza?" Amanda asked. "Why would you ask that?"

Mickey went over to Arno and clapped him on the back. "You may be looking for Kelli, but I don't think she's looking for you." Liza continued to stand only a few feet from Arno. Mickey went downstairs.

Kelli, meanwhile, was pretending Arno wasn't

calling her name. She stood with Randall and his two friends. She began to do a sort of shimmy dance. Arno watched her. He thought she looked graceful and smooth. Randall and his friends were clapping.

"I need to talk to you," Arno said. He'd crept closer, and now his clothes seemed to be dripping off him, his shirt hanging down over his suit pants. Arno knew something was happening to him, but he couldn't figure out what it was. He had no idea what to call it.

"I'm busy now," Kelli said. "Can't you see I'm dancing?" But then she turned to Arno anyway, and grabbed him by the shoulders and kissed him hard on the lips. She said, "That's for taking me to Florida." Then she went back to dancing. Jonathan came down the stairs, but he stayed back and only watched.

"I'll bring you anywhere you want to go," Arno said to Kelli.

"Yeah?" Randall said. He inserted himself between Arno and Kelli. "What's your point?"

"Because I love you!" Arno yelled as he pushed Randall out of the way. He couldn't help it. Randall sort of staggered, but Arno didn't see him. He'd finally figured out what to call what he was feeling.

"Come on," Kelli said. She had white eyeliner around her eyes and her lipstick seemed to do a neon flicker in the light from the Floods' chandelier.

"No, I really do."

Jonathan and David stood with Liza and Amanda. They watched Kelli and Arno in silence.

"If you love me," Kelli said loudly, "then why did you fool around with Amanda half an hour after you met me?"

David, who'd been in the middle of a sip of beer, sagged suddenly. Out of the corner of his eyes, Arno saw.

"David, I'm sorry," Arno said. But David only turned and went up the stairs.

"I'm going up to the roof," Liza announced, to nobody in particular. Arno saw her look back a couple of times, but he couldn't meet her eyes. So Liza strode up the staircase.

"Are you all right?" Jonathan asked Liza. He sort of half-grabbed her leg as she passed.

"Get off," she said, and kicked at him.

"Huh?" Jonathan asked.

"Dude, you need to chill," Kelli said to Arno. "You're losing friends by the second."

Arno shook his head. He felt so confused.

"Yeah. Let it go," Randall said.

But it was too late. Arno had dropped down on both knees and his eyes were closed. He raised his hands up and clasped them together.

"Love me," he said. "I'll do anything."

"Oh, man," Kelli said. "Like I don't have a boyfriend back home who's quarterback of our football team and could kick all your asses!" And she laughed. "Jonathan, didn't you tell your friends that? I mean, I'd have thought you would've."

"Say what?" Jonathan asked. Arno opened his eyes and glanced up at the staircase, where Jonathan had taken a seat after Liza kicked at him.

"That doesn't matter," Arno said. "Nothing could compete with what I feel for you."

"But Arno," Kelli said. "I don't want to be tied down. I just got here. I'm just getting started."

I get arno out of there

I got down to where Arno was and I tried to pull him up, before he could think too clearly about what Kelli had said, but he struggled away from me. It was both extremely weird and no surprise at all that Arno had met his match in Kelli, but this was obviously the wrong time to comment on it.

"Kelli, you never told me about any boyfriend at home," I said. And as soon as the words came out of my mouth I knew they had about as much value as Arno's humiliating love plea.

"I don't care about your boyfriend," Arno said. "Stay here and let's live together."

"Where?" I asked. "In your room at your parents' house? Are you insane? Come with me."

And then I literally dragged Arno out to the front stoop. When I looked back, I could see Kelli looking at me, and she gave me a big wink. I just shook my head. *Thanks for letting me come out with you*, she'd said. I remembered how simple that had sounded, cut with a hint of country. And now, among other things, she'd destroyed my friend.

Arno let out a moan.

"It'll be okay," I said.

Out on the stoop the night was surprisingly warm. I looked back behind me and realized that the party was growing. We hadn't even begun to look for Patch.

Arno plopped down on the steps and put his head in his hands. "Dude, what am I going to do?"

I kind of patted him on the shoulder, which felt ridiculous. Some girls walked up the steps and stared at him like, *that's Arno*? They shook their heads in amazement and went inside.

"She's wrong for you," I said.

"I love her."

I took a deep breath. "Arno," I said, "Kelli's a user. She could never love you. Look what she just did to you in there."

I figured the truth would make him sit bolt upright or something. But his head stayed down around his knees.

"I don't care," he said. "Nobody ever made me

feel like that before."

"Can you be more specific?" I asked, and then when he looked up, I wished I hadn't. I remembered back in fifth grade, when he'd figured out that if he let them, most girls would make out with him, even girls like Molly, who supposedly liked other boys, like David.

"Most times girls come up and they smile and they say whatever junk they like to say and I pretend to listen and then we fool around. I don't even have to be coherent."

"But Kelli wasn't like that."

"Right."

"She played you is why."

"No—dude, it was more than that."

"Then why did she just humiliate you and now she's downstairs with some hot-shit artist and you're out on the stoop crying on my shoulder?"

"There's something else," Arno said.

"About Amanda? She's pissed is what I figure. She thought she was blowing off David for you and you were going to step up and go out with her in a real way. As soon as I'm done with you I've got to go find David."

"No," Arno said. "This other thing is as bad or worse."

I stepped back then, and wrapped my hands around the iron railing. I'd flashed on a vision of Arno with Flan. No, I didn't even need to take it there—them together in a room talking, that was enough. Flan would complain to him about my unwillingness to be with her and Arno would fix that as he slipped her tank top off her shoulders.

"What could be worse?" I asked. There were icicles between my toes. Icicles or razors.

"I fooled around with Liza."

"Really," I said. And I knew there was more wonder in my voice than anger. Liza was my friend. And probably she was in pain, which explained that whole other aspect of what had just happened.

"You're in trouble," I said.

"I know," Arno said. "I'm starting to wonder if David was right. If Patch were around, none of this would have happened. Anyway, I don't understand who I am now that I'm in love. What can I do to make things better?"

I didn't tell him that was ridiculous. The music had gone up inside the house. I knew that we had to get out of there and find Patch before someone else decided to be in love with Kelli.

"I'll figure something out," I said.

david gets a nice surprise

After David had heard what Kelli said to Arno, he'd wandered upstairs and eventually found himself sitting on an old leather couch in the Floods' library on the third floor in the back, where the walls were covered with Frederick Flood's collection of nineteenth-century nude photographs. The room brought back good memories for David, because the five friends used to sneak in there when they were in middle school, and they'd spend hours viewing the collection.

Now David sat quietly and took it all in again. Since he'd last been in the room, Mr. Flood had collected a whole bunch of old globes that lit up from the inside, and there were tons of art books stacked on low tables. David had his hood over his head. He should have known it was Arno all along. He'd just been unwilling to admit it. He hadn't even gotten to the part about figuring out who convinced whom to fool around with whom. Then the door clicked open. David looked up. Kelli stood there.

"You know what you remind me of?" Kelli asked as she closed the door behind her.

"No, what?" He figured she'd probably say Kenny, from *South Park*. Everyone else did. And he didn't think she knew about the Most Sensitive Guy in the World thing.

"Just a really good guy. Like a Harrison Ford's costar type. Like Josh Hartnett, with the square jaw."

"Thanks, I guess."

"Your only problem is your ex-girlfriend Amanda is a total bitch."

"She is not," David said, but his heart wasn't in it. He knew she kind of was. She'd fooled around with one of his best friends. But he loved her anyway. He understood that love could be that way—he hadn't been brought up by a pair of therapists for nothing.

"And she's not my girlfriend. I broke up with her after she cheated on me." But when he said it, he realized there was a part missing, and it rang hollow. "Arno. She cheated on me with Arno."

"I'm sorry it came out the way it did," Kelli said. "You can talk to me about how you feel if you want to."

So David told her the story, about how he'd fallen in love with Amanda and how they'd had such an amazing time together, and yet at the same time how she always felt kind of out of his reach. And by the end of it, Kelli had her feet up in David's lap and they were both drinking from the same extra large mug of rum and Coke that Kelli had brought upstairs with her.

"You know what," Kelli said. "You really are a sensitive guy. Maybe not in the whole world, but you know, you're sensitive."

"Stop," David said.

"You don't even want to beat up Arno?"

"Sure I do."

Kelli just shook her head. It looked as if she were thinking. Then she stood up and went to the door.

"Don't," David said.

"Don't what?"

"Don't leave."

She smiled. She turned off the overhead lights, and turned up the lights in the globes.

"It feels like we're floating in the middle of the Milky Way," David whispered.

She came back to the couch and sat down.

"I've so totally wanted to hook up in New York," Kelli said.

"You haven't?"

"Nope," she said. "Not once."

And she was really close to David. He could smell her warm skin and he was reminded of that first night when he met her, how he just had this kind of instamatic crush on her. Not like with Amanda, where she had to keep saying no till she'd gone away for the summer and then she came back and sort of begrudgingly fell in love. This was different, he thought. And he was kissing her.

"Not with anybody?" he asked.

"Nobody," she said, and sort of laughed. "I was never going to go anywhere with Randall Oddy. He's so weird, and so much older."

She got up again, and this time she put a chair against the door.

"Wow," David said. "Some people could say I'm doing this just to get back at Amanda and Arno."

"Shut up," Kelli said. They'd fallen onto the rug, which was thick and purple. The globes glowed above them.

"Take off your sweatshirt," Kelli said. "I think that thing's been holding you back. I don't think you should wear it anymore."

"I will if you take off your shirt," David said.

"I already did. Can't you see?"

"Oh," David said. "Oh yeah."

i go head-to-head with february

I went down to the kitchen to find David and Mickey. A bunch of February Flood's friends were eating at the table. They'd thrown away our leftovers and were having their own feast of food that had been ordered in from Odeon—roast chicken and fish and plastic dishes of spinach and carrots. February had taken over one side of the table. She was wearing a spiked dog collar and picking her teeth with a bone from what looked like the remains of a trout.

"Sit down, Jonathan," she said.

"Why?"

"Do it." And her friends suddenly got up, chicken legs and tuna steaks in hand, and drifted away. So I sat down across from February, and started eating some of someone's sweet potato fries.

"What's up with you and Flan?"

"Why do you ask?"

"Because when she called just now she said she wasn't coming home if you were here."

"Where is she?"

"She didn't say."

"But I didn't do anything," I said, as if that were true or relevant.

"And I'd thought you went out with Liza, but when I came downstairs, Liza was looking all upset, and she says it's because she got with that moron Arno, which I don't really think she would've done if she were with you. So from that I figured out that you lied to my little sister."

"Um," I said.

"You certainly hang out with her a lot," February said.

"But she's in eighth grade. We're like—buddies."

"Buddies? Because she's in eighth grade? What are you talking about? When I was in eighth grade I was sleeping with the drummer from the Strokes."

"That's you, February," I said. "Flan is different."

"That's what I'm worried about."

Then we just stared at each other. February took a sip of Jack Daniels from the bottle. I suspected this would be the last coherent conversation she had tonight.

"Anyway, it's no big deal, I heard some other

guy is after her," February said.

"Other guy?" I asked.

"Like that's an alien concept? You and your bunch of idiots aren't the only ones in this town who know how to get girls."

By then a few people had drifted into the kitchen, including Mickey, who seemed sort of unfocused. But he was smiling. Philippa was with him. They were such a good couple—they were always happy when they were together.

"Hey, February," Mickey said. She handed the Jack Daniels to Mickey. He took a long hit.

"Listen," February said to me. "Here's an idea. I'll put in a good word for you with my little sister if you get the hell out of here and go find Patch. How's that sound?"

"Why do I need help with Flan?" I asked.

"Oh, believe me," February said. "You need help."

"Let's go get Arno and David," Mickey said.

We went up the stairs to the main room. They were blasting the new Nas up there, and February's friends were slam dancing.

We heard some high-pitched girlish yelling coming from the back porch.

"Sounds like Arno aggravated another girl," I said.

Arno had been looking around for Kelli for the last ten minutes. She'd totally disappeared. Deep down, he was able to deduce that, based on his own similar disappearances at parties, she was fooling around with somebody. Though it was warm inside, his teeth chattered. He'd left his jacket somewhere and now he stood there in his suit pants, his white shirt hanging out, holding a bottle of Grolsch and shivering.

"Could I speak to you?" Liza asked.

They stood in the back parlor on the main floor, overlooking the lighted garden.

"Um, sure," Arno said. He didn't look at her.

"You're really hot on that Kelli girl, huh?"

"I guess so," Arno said. "Yeah. I am." He glanced at her quickly to see if maybe—even though they'd practically crawled under the booth and had sex at the Corner Bistro less than three hours ago—she felt some sympathy for how intensely he was crushing on another girl.

"Not what I wanted to hear," Liza said.

Then she poked Arno hard in the ribs.

"Ow," Arno said. "Look, Liza, I'm sorry about what we . . . did. But I didn't mean to—"

"You called me!"

"Yeah, but—"

"And I fell for it. Do you know how that makes me feel?"

"I'm sorry," Arno said. "I really am."

Then Arno saw Jonathan and Mickey standing in the massive open doors to the living room. Behind them the room was pretty empty and quiet except for the sound system, which was pumping.

"You're a jerk, Arno Wildenburger!" Liza screamed. And then she kicked Arno right in what he and his friends liked to call "the gentles."

She was wearing the black boots she always wore. Arno yelped, grabbed his suit pants, and crumpled to the floor like a half-empty sack of pinto beans.

"Oof," Arno said.

"Liza—" Jonathan began to say.

"You shut up," Liza yelled. But then she turned around and she was hanging around Jonathan's neck and crying.

Arno heard Jonathan whisper "five minutes" to Mickey, who was carefully helping him off the floor. "Then we go find Patch."

"Yeah, let's find Patch," Arno croaked.

mickey rounds up the rest of the gang

Finally, the three of them made for the door. And sure, Mickey knew that Jonathan and Arno were as much running away from a whole bunch of girl problems as they were going to find their buddy, but that didn't mean the search was a bad idea.

Mickey had filled a thermos with what he was calling "Patch Punch." Arno was having trouble walking so he'd borrowed a silver-tipped cane from Mr. Flood's umbrella stand. Each boy had his cell phone and some cash, courtesy of Mr. and Mrs. Flood. They'd helped themselves from the big laughing Buddha jar in the Floods' bedroom, which was where everyone knew to go to get money. They figured it was fair to use Flood money to find a Flood son, after all.

"Let's go," Mickey said. He was wearing aviator goggles, and the pants of his jumpsuit were rolled up high.

"Ready," Jonathan said.

"Ready," Arno said. But he didn't sound that way.

"Let's go!" Mickey yelled again.

"Wait," Jonathan said. "Where's David?"

And of course that was when all three of them figured out at the same moment that David had been missing and so had Kelli and that meant something. But nobody said it aloud—because it would be painful for Arno to hear and, after all, he'd already been kicked in the gentles.

They stood on the stoop. Nobody really wanted to go back in the house.

"February is going to kick out all those sophomores in about five minutes," Jonathan said. "We don't want to be around for that."

"Shit," Mickey said. "I'll go."

They weren't in the parlor, so Mickey hit the top floor first, but nobody was up there except for a pair of February's friends who were finishing their chicken dinner in the middle of Mr. and Mrs. Flood's massive four-poster bed.

"David," he yelled. He tried the third floor, where people rarely went, because it was just the library and the maid's quarters and a family room that was basically used as storage space. Mickey sniffed around. Things were too quiet.

"Coming," David said. Mickey heard this as a kind of muffled cry. Without thinking he pushed open the door to the library. A chair fell over. David and Kelli were putting their clothes back in place.

"Ooh," Mickey said.

"Hi," Kelli said back.

David looked at Mickey and sort of bit his lower lip. Mickey nodded and said, "We have to go find Patch. You want me to make them wait for a few minutes?"

"No," David said. He turned and kissed Kelli once on the cheek. She smiled at him.

"We've got to find our friend," David said.

"That's cool," Kelli said. "Is Randall Oddy still downstairs? I promised I'd hang out with him."

Mickey rolled his eyes at David, who only shrugged.

david and arno don't deal with each other

"David . . . ," Arno began.

"Dude," David said, "I don't want to deal with you right now. We have more important things to do."

Their first stop was Local 13 on West 13th Street, where Patch sometimes went to score weed from a bartender called Tuddy. But the four boys couldn't get in because they didn't have any girls with them.

"No problem," David said. "Let me take care of this."

"What?" Jonathan asked.

Mickey and Arno were busy just then, ogling a model who was ogling them back. With Arno in his jacket and Mickey in his jumpsuit and goggles they looked like a Polo ad gone berserk.

"I'm going to slip by you and check in with Tuddy, for five minutes," David told the bouncer, who was some kind of ex-pro wrestler.

"No," the bouncer said. But David just stood there, a cool smile on his face. Waiting.

"Fine, in to see Tuddy." The bouncer held the door open. David patted Jonathan on the back as he slipped into the club, as if to say, get ready for the new me.

Inside Local 13, David brushed against a girl who was dancing with some girlfriends. The place was entirely blue—blue walls, tables, chairs, ceiling, lights. They could get away with it because the people were so good-looking.

"'Scuse me, baby," he said, just to see how it sounded.

"Don't worry about it," the girl said, and ran her hand over his chest. David smiled. Yeah, the new me.

"No, I haven't seen him," Tuddy said when David got to him. "But I've got fifty grams of something special I grew myself—"

"No, thanks," David said. "Right now I'm high on life."

"That's weird," Tuddy said. He rubbed his shaved head for a second. David had met Tuddy once or twice before.

"What is?"

"You didn't sound like a total idiot when you said that."

"Yeah, man," David said. "I'm in a good place right now." David smiled and began to go back the way he came.

"Hey, where you going?" the girl he'd brushed by asked when he attempted to brush by again.

"Where do you want me to be going?" David asked.

"Nowhere fast."

"Sounds fair," David said. He started to dance with the girl.

"I like your hoodie," she said.

"You should see what's underneath."

"You're bold," the girl said. "I'm Chloe."

She poked him in the chest while they danced and David grabbed her hand and bit the tip of her finger lightly.

"Ooh," the girl said.

"You remind me of somebody when you say that."

They kept dancing. David thought, *I'm tall and handsome.* And for the second time in his life, David forgot his friends.

the search party rests for the night

"I don't think David's coming out," Mickey said.

"You may be right," I said. "What the hell is going on with him?"

"He got with that Ooh girl, and now he thinks he's the shit," Mickey said. He was only looking at me when he said it, but I could feel Arno next to me. He was right there and then a second later, it was like *ppphht*. He'd deflated.

"He did it to get back at me," Arno said. "No wonder he hasn't bothered to confront me. He's playing a complex psychological game with my feelings."

"Um," Mickey said. "I think maybe that wasn't totally nice of me to say out loud, but when I saw those two together, I didn't think they were thinking about your feelings at all."

"I wish your cousin would go home," Arno said. "I can't stand having her around and I love her so much."

"If there was a person exchange somewhere, and we could go there and trade Kelli for Patch," I said, "believe me, I'd do it."

I looked around and there were twenty people or so milling around the velvet rope, and since they had nothing better to do, they were staring at us. Because, as far as I was concerned, we were younger and cooler than they were.

"Let's just go. I don't know what he's up to but it's been half an hour," Mickey said.

So we began to walk east. I think we all knew one thing, which was that we had absolutely no clue where Patch was. Then I heard this sniffling noise next to me. I looked over and Arno was crying. Crying? Arno? I threw my arm around him.

"Dude, I'm going home. I think we should call the cops," Arno said through his tears.

"Stop it," I said. I mean, it was one thing for David to cry, but for Arno—that was too much. "Get a grip!"

"We're not calling anybody yet," Mickey said. "We've got about thirty hours. And I'm going to find him. I've got some hunches."

I looked over at Arno. Mickey was barely allowed back in school and he was still swinging around his cast. Maybe he did have some hunches. But I couldn't imagine what they were.

"Well, I need to go to sleep," Arno said. I checked my watch. It was about three in the morning. I yawned.

"You've hit bottom," I said to Arno. "I promise things won't get any worse for you."

"Thanks," Arno said, and it sounded like he meant it.

We walked over to Fifth Avenue and just sort of stood there. Some cabs went by and I knew I should probably shovel Arno into one and call it quits myself. We'd find Patch tomorrow, for sure. There were people's houses we hadn't checked, kids at boarding school we hadn't called, ice cream parlors we hadn't visited.

Then a big black Chevy SUV drove by really slowly. Mickey saw it and before Arno or I could say anything, he jumped on the fender.

"I'm going to go home to get my Vespa and tool around," Mickey yelled.

"Is that a good idea?" I asked as we watched him disappear around the corner. His goggles were on and his jumpsuit was rolled up at the wrists and ankles. He curled himself around his cast and he looked as if he were going to take off like some kind of superhero.

"Well, that takes care of him," I said. "Let's get you home."

"I'm sorry about what I've been doing," Arno said.

"It's cool," I said. "I'm sure you'll do something that will make everyone like you again."

"Really?" Arno looked up at me. His black hair was sticking out in all directions and his eyes were dried out and puffy. But he was still a really good-looking guy. Anyone could see that. I really didn't believe he'd meant to do as much harm as he had.

"Well, if you don't think of anything, I'll make up something nice for you to do," I said.

"Thanks."

Arno was still sniffling when I packed him in the back of a cab and said goodnight to him. He said something I couldn't understand to the driver, who immediately smiled and began to chatter.

"What's that?" I asked.

"Farsi," Arno said. "Kinda neat, huh? I learned it from David. I really hope we can still be friends."

saturday morning, sunny, sixty degrees

mickey pardo, p.i.

Mickey came to on a torn velvet couch in the back of Save The Robots. He'd have checked his watch if he'd had one. Save The Robots was a revival of an old East Village after-hours club where people went to do drugs and doze. And this was definitely after hours. He looked around him, and he knew the gray light that came in at the sides of the blacked-out windows was the dawn. He heard a scratching noise and checked his cast, which he'd been ignoring. A mouse was gnawing on it.

I should jump, Mickey thought. But he didn't. There was a brown drink cradled next to him on the ugly sofa. Guinness? Maybe. He took a sip and spat it out, whatever it was. Man, was his dad ever going to kill him. That is, assuming that his dad hadn't gone out to Montauk the day before, or the day before that. He wished he kept better track of these things. No, wait. He'd had dinner with his dad last night. Shit. Maybe they'd gone to Montauk after dinner?

He looked around him and saw little knots of people

talking, still awake, incredibly. And then he recognized someone. Randall Oddy was there with some guys and a few women and a young girl who had a lot more energy than anyone else. Ooh. Mickey stood up. If he could have connected the dots, he would have. But the last thing he remembered was hanging off the back of an SUV and making a sharp right into the East Village. Then . . . that was it.

"Hi!" Kelli said.

"Ooh," Mickey said.

"Enough with that," Kelli said.

"I didn't mean—" but Mickey stopped. He'd meant Ooh, there's a mouse on the floor near your feet. But he wasn't ready to explain that, not just yet. If Kelli was the kind of girl who could have a mouse nibbling on the fringe of her leather boot and not notice, that was her problem.

"Come and sit with me and Randall and the gang," Kelli said. "We were just discussing the right place to get some food. I'm sick to death of Florent."

"You're tired of Florent? You've been here a week and a half!" Mickey said. "Calvin Klein's been here for about ninety years and he still goes to Florent."

"I know," Kelli said as she shook the mouse off her foot. "I was talking to him about that last time I was there."

Kelli had Mickey by the hand and she led him to sit down with Randall Oddy and his crowd. They were all discussing who'd been accepted into the Whitney Biennial art show. Mickey watched Kelli nod intensely, as if she had a clue what they were talking about.

"*Man*," Mickey said. He'd looked down and he had a notepad with a bunch of information on it. This notepad told him two things—that he'd actually spent some time researching where Patch had gone, and that he'd done a lousy, drunken job of it. Because the words on the page looked like nonsense—they could have been in Farsi for all he could make of them.

"I'm sorry about last night," Randall Oddy said. Mickey brought him into focus. Oh, he thought. This clown.

"It's cool," Mickey said.

"What's that?" Randall Oddy asked. And he and his friends all gathered around to see Mickey's pad.

"Cool," someone said.

"Look," Mickey said. "I know all you art guys think these are like my little drawings and whatever, but the truth is my buddy Patch is missing. And clearly I wrote all these notes about it last night, but because I'm on, um, pain medication, now I see that they're gibberish. So it's not what you think."

"Not art," Oddy said.

214

"No."

"What did you say your friend's name was?"

"Patch. Patch Flood."

"Funny name."

"So is yours."

"You know something?" another guy asked. He had a high voice and his hair was all down in front of his face. "I think I've heard that name recently, at Graca's house."

"Graca?" Kelli asked. Even Mickey could tell she didn't like the sound of another woman's name. A hush surrounded the group.

"If your friend is who I think he is," the high-voiced guy said, "he's the luckiest guy in the world."

"That's him," Mickey said. "No doubt."

what do you wear to a search party?

I met David at his house on Saturday morning and we caught a cab to Barneys.

"This is crazy," he said, but it was the fifth time he'd said it, so I ignored him. He kept staring out the window as if he were seeing Manhattan for the first time.

We got up to Barneys and of course I had to keep reminding myself that this shopping trip wasn't for me. It was for David. He'd called me around nine on Saturday morning. I was planning not to move till at least noon, but then he'd said he needed to get some cool clothes. That perked me up, I'll admit, but I still went back to sleep for a while. I was fairly sure that Kelli hadn't arrived home yet. Our mothers were away again, staying with old family friends, the Caufields, at their estate in Westchester.

"What you're looking for," I said to David, "are clothes that give a nod to what a terrific, all-

American basketball-playing guy with a sensitive streak you are, but still say hey, I know how to put on a pair of pants. Do you see that?"

"The thing that I realized last night," David said, "is that I'm still in love with Amanda."

"Oh," I said. I couldn't even remember when I'd last seen Amanda. Who had she gone off with? I could ask Liza, but no. Was Liza even my friend anymore? And Arno? My foot began to shake uncontrollably.

"I know that, deep inside. I didn't know it when I was fooling around with your cousin, but later, when I was fooling around with that girl at the club, I knew it. And she did, too."

"What about Arno?" I asked.

"He's in love with Kelli, right?"

"Yeah," I said. "He was last night, anyway."

"Then maybe he's suffered enough."

We were up at Barneys by then and we both hopped out, but we didn't go around the corner to the doors to the men's side. I like to go through all the women's stuff on the ground floor, because a lot of those women who offer you perfume and stuff are hot.

"How'd the girl at the club know you were in love with someone else?"

"We were kissing, and she said, 'I can feel that you're thinking about someone else.'"

"Maybe you're just a lousy kisser," I said, because we'd arrived at men's sweaters and I was suddenly distracted. It smelled like fall in there, of cashmere, of deep browns and leafy reds. The glass cases glittered at me like great chunks of rock candy.

"Shut up, dude. I need to change for Amanda. It's like, I can't always be brooding all the time and acting so, so self-indulgent."

"Uh-huh," I said. We were passing some new John Varvatos jackets and I couldn't listen to David anymore right then.

"So that's why we're here. So I can change."

"I see." I drifted onto the third floor, and we checked out the sneakers. David chose a pair of Miu-Miu slip-ons and asked for his size. We sat down on the squishy leather and rubber chairs and waited.

"You've really helped me to discover who I am," David said. "Thanks for that."

"Honest?" I asked. I squinted at him. I couldn't remember doing anything like that. I'd actually been sitting there wondering if I could slip away from him and go down and check out the new

Crockett and Jones slip-ons in the loafer area. But I wasn't sure that was such a good idea—considering I'd bought a pair of shoes *yesterday*.

"What about Kelli?" I asked as I stood up. "You didn't have sex with her, did you?"

"No—we didn't get very far either. She told me I was in love with Amanda, too."

"Wow," I said. "You are awfully sensitive."

A guy was coming over with his sneakers and I left David then. I was pretty well amazed at what a good mood he was in, but fooling around with two girls in one night and waking up in love with your ex-girlfriend can have that effect. It was a very cake-and-eat-it-too kind of feeling, I imagine.

I went over to the Crockett and Jones display. So expensive. But also so cool. I shook my head and went for my credit card.

"Can I help you with that?"

I looked up from the display and there was this girl there. She was probably nineteen—and was clearly one of those girls who went to Barnard and worked two or three shifts at Barneys during the week, because the commissions are outrageous, and she was pretty in a pink-sweater-with-pink-cardigan-over-it kind of way. "Really, can I help you?"

"I don't know," I said. She was shorter than me, and she had these great bangs, cut high over her wide almond eyes. I had this weird thing happen to my head then, as if somehow I was not just discovering this girl, but had always known her.

"I've seen you here before," she said. "I'm Fernanda."

"I'm Jonathan," I said. We shook hands. She smelled of something really good involving daisies. The store got real quiet then, and I think the noise I was hearing was like a harp or a mandolin. At that moment, David moon-walked by us in his new shoes.

"I love these!" he yelled. The salesman who was helping him was clapping and doing a human beat box routine. But I was completely focused on Fernanda.

"You like shoes," she said.

"Yeah," I admitted.

"Sometimes after the store closes for the day, or early, before we open the doors, I like to come over to the men's section and just hang out. I bet you'd enjoy that."

"Oh yeah," I said. "I really would."

We were totally grinning at each other like

idiots. *Soul mate.* And then, while David picked out a couple more pairs of cool shoes, Fernanda and I exchanged numbers.

"There's a party tonight," she said. "I'll call you and let you know where it is."

"Thanks," I said.

David and I left, and went down to check out khakis for him.

My phone rang. Mickey.

"I know where Patch is," Mickey said.

"You do? Did you just find out?"

"No, it was this morning, really early."

"So why'd you wait till now to tell us?" I asked. David pulled on my shirt. I pointed at the phone and crossed my eyes.

"Because he's in a good place," Mickey said. "And I just woke up. Why don't you guys come over here around six or so and we'll have some drinks and then go get him."

"What about your dad?"

"I'm pretty sure he's in Montauk."

"You want anything?" I asked, because I was suddenly feeling really happy. "We're at Barneys."

"No, you freakish clothes-hound, I don't want anything from Barneys," Mickey said, and ended the call.

"Mickey found Patch!"

"That's good news," David said. He held up a pinstripe running suit from Marc Jacobs. "I'm going to get the sneakers, but I don't think I'm going to buy this. If I do, they'll never let me back on the basketball team."

arno goes back to what he's good at

Arno spent most of Saturday afternoon in his room, watching George Clooney movies. He knew he didn't have quite that kind of style, not yet anyway. But he liked watching *Ocean's 11*. He liked the attitudes and he loved the idea of being very smart in a criminal-minded sort of way.

He lay on the floor and did crunches, what felt like hundreds of them, and quoted Clooney's lines. He thought of Kelli. If only she'd return his pages and calls. He lay on his side then and squeezed his eyes shut to hold back the tears that he simply couldn't believe were coming.

His home phone rang. Jonathan.

"Mickey found Patch. We're meeting over at his house in two hours."

"What about Kelli?"

"What about her?"

"Is she coming?"

"Um, no? I have no idea where she is. Mickey found

Patch, aren't you psyched?"

"Yeah," Arno said. He went to his closet and pulled out a candy-striped button-down that practically glowed. Happy shirt.

"I guess I'll keep calling her."

"Yeah, you do that," Jonathan said. "And we'll see you before seven, got it?"

After Jonathan ended the call, Arno tried to reach Kelli again. Nothing. He knew she was leaving the next morning at eleven, with her mom. He could go to St. Louis. He'd have to rent a car and find a place to stay, and miss more school. Somewhere underneath his love for her, he felt as if she'd stolen his cool, and he was annoyed about that. He even wondered, if he hadn't seen her, would he have fooled around with Amanda and Liza?

"Arno?" his mother called. The Wildenburgers were having a dinner party, as usual, and his mother was stopping by on her way to the kitchen, where she had to supervise the staff. She stood in the doorway in black silk pants and a black cashmere sweater, not yet in her eveningwear. "Come and taste the soup, won't you, dear? It's lobster bisque."

So Arno went with her, because he couldn't think of a reason to say no, or start a fight. They walked down the long hallway and halfway there his mother was called away by a maid—Arno's dad was on the phone. But Arno kept going toward the kitchen. He figured he'd eat some of whatever they had—if he could get in there before they wrapped the prosciutto around the figs, maybe he could make a ham sandwich.

The kitchen was as massive as everything else, all white enamel and buffed steel and butcher block, and there were three cooks busily preparing dinner for twelve. Arno saw some medallions of veal and edged toward them.

"Those are for the guests, sir," a woman said. Arno looked up, with a twinge of annoyance, thinking, *my kitchen.*

The girl who stared back at him was clearly a server and looked not much older than a college sophomore, probably at NYU.

"I live here," Arno said.

"Oh?" she said. She stood in front of him, and she was in tight blue jeans and a hooded sweatshirt. She held her uniform, a white button-down shirt and black tuxedo pants, on a hanger. A Latina girl with sharp features and big black eyes. To Arno, she looked awfully precise. She was staring at him. He couldn't tell if she was annoyed or what. Meanwhile, the three male cooks were busily moving around, cooking. The girl kept staring at Arno.

"Yeah," Arno said. "In fact, my bedroom's back down

that hallway."

"Oh, it is?"

"Yeah, in case you need to get dressed and you want to get away from all these guys. I've got a bathroom back there and everything. I've got a big shower with this tiled chair thing in it."

"That sounds nice," she said. Her voice was low. He realized that maybe she was older. Twenty-four? Wow, maybe she didn't even go to college.

"You should see it," Arno said. "Even if you don't want to change back there."

The woman glanced back at the cooks, who were busily stirring the bisque.

"Coming!" Arno's mother yelled. She'd gone around the back way toward the kitchen. The cooks immediately looked up. One made bug eyes at the other, as if to say, *the crazy lady's on her way*. Immediately, all the cooks got to looking even busier. They started chattering in French.

"Let's go," Arno said. "Before you have to deal with my mom."

Arno grabbed the girl and a chunk of beef tenderloin with his other hand and they ran back down the corridor to his room. The girl was laughing. They got back to his room and Arno closed the door behind him.

"This is great of you to give me this place to change,"

the girl said. "I'm Mariela."

"I'm Arno."

They held out their hands to each other. Both Arno's home phone and cell phone were ringing. He ignored them. Dead Prez was blaring out of the stereo. Arno turned the music off.

"Where's the bathroom?" Mariela asked. Arno pointed and they were kissing on his bed before he'd had time to put his hand down.

"It'll be easier to change," Arno said, "if you've got your clothes off."

"Mmm."

"I've got to change clothes, too, actually."

"Oh yeah?"

"You might want to take a shower," Arno said, "before you have to work. I was going to take one myself."

"That sounds good."

There was silence for a few minutes. Arno felt his room transformed, floating away on a cloud.

"I'm back," Arno said, mostly to himself.

"Yes, you are," Mariela said.

"Arno!" His mom called out from somewhere down the hall. "One of the servers is lost! Is she in your room?"

"Yeah, Mom. She spilled something on her white shirt, so I'm giving her one of mine."

"That's nice, dear."

mickey shouldn't be driving

"I can't find my Vespa anywhere," Mickey yelled. He was sort of shaky on his feet, since he'd had only about four hours of not-very-good sleep. He wandered around his dad's studio, looking behind sculptures and workstations, but the Vespa seemed to be lost.

"Where'd you see it last?" Caselli asked.

Mickey stared at him. Caselli had been working for Ricardo Pardo since before Mickey was born. He wore the same white jumpsuit that all of Ricardo's employees wore, but his had a black dot on the chest, which signified that he was the leader, the head guy. He was also kind of Mickey's godfather.

"Dude," Mickey said. "I have no idea where it is, and my friends are coming over pretty soon, I think and . . . it'd be nice to have it."

"You're in no condition to drive anything," Caselli said.

"Dude . . . I found Patch."

"What does that mean?"

But Mickey had already turned around and walked back to his room. He had about a thousand in cash stashed in the belly of a blowfish his father had brought back from a fishing trip off the coast of Japan. He went to find the blowfish, which hung by a piece of twine from a pipe above his head. But because he was standing under it, he couldn't see it. Instead, he found a thick envelope from American Express under several letters from school, which he'd really need to deal with, and soon. The letter had a credit card in it.

"Cool," Mickey said. He decided to look for the cash later, took the card, and walked out of the house. "Tell my friends to chill here till I get back."

"Wait," Caselli said. "Where are you going?"

But Mickey was already out the door. He grabbed a cab and shot over to Crosby Street, where he went into Vespa Global.

"Hi, Mickey," the manager said. "Come back to pick up your helmet?"

"I'll take the black one," Mickey said.

"We have only white helmets."

"And two gallons of gas." Mickey was already sitting on his new bike. He drew out his new credit card and flipped it to the manager.

Mickey found his phone in his jumpsuit pocket and called Philippa.

"I found Patch," Mickey said. "Meet me outside your place."

It was all the manager could do to get the door open, get Mickey to drag a pen across the signature line on the form, and get out of the way.

Mickey adjusted his goggles and tied a handkerchief over his mouth so he wouldn't swallow any bugs. He tore down one-way streets the wrong way, popped curbs, and shot between pedestrians. At Philippa's house, he honked. It sounded like *Oooot, Oooot*.

She came outside. She was in a flowery dress and her hair brushed against her shoulders. She sat down on her stoop. He loved her.

"I love you," he said.

"Then get off the bike."

"No, I need it. I found Patch."

"Where is he?"

"I think . . . somewhere in Chinatown."

"Look, Mickey, I love you, too. But if you don't get off the bike and walk home, I'm not speaking to you. You're in no position to have an engine under your ass."

"Come with me."

"I don't think so. Listen, if you don't straighten up at least a little, we can't go out. You can't wind up in the hospital every weekend. It's too insane."

Mickey looked closer and Philippa's beautiful gray

eyes seemed to be wet around the edges.

"I'll change," Mickey said.

"Give me the bike."

"After we find Patch and we get that Ooh girl back to Alabama or wherever she's from, I'll change. I swear I will."

"Well, she does need to get out of town. I can't think of anybody who didn't get messed up by her and it's only a matter of time before she comes after you. But wait—"

But Mickey shot off, toward his house. His friends were there and he had responsibilities. He tore around corners, riding almost parallel to the ground. He shot down Seventh Avenue and weaved between the thick Saturday afternoon traffic headed toward the Holland Tunnel and New Jersey. Drivers honked and threw lit cigarettes and newspapers at him. He didn't notice.

Caselli stood in the doorway to his house, and he clearly was fretting. Mickey got off the bike and Caselli caught it.

"Your friends are here," Caselli said.

Mickey pulled off the handkerchief and then groped in his pocket for a tissue or something to wipe his nose. Instead, he found a cocktail napkin. Something on it caught his eye before he put it to his face. An IOU written in lipstick, with the imprint of a kiss.

"Oh shit," Mickey said. "I remember now. I gave my Vespa to this girl last night so she'd stop bugging me for a kiss."

He started to laugh. Caselli did, too, but his laugh was a bit more concerned.

"Arno's in your room," Caselli said.

Mickey made his way upstairs slowly. He knew it would be pretty hard to get that new Vespa away from Caselli.

"Mickey!"

Arno had been going through Mickey's CDs, looking for something to play.

"Let's go get Patch!" Arno yelled.

"What about David?" asked Mickey. "Where is he? And where's Jonathan?"

"I need to apologize to David, too, now that I'm feeling good," Arno said. He was on one of Mickey's skateboards and he was tacking around the room, knocking into things.

"I can see that," Mickey said. "Look, I've got a new Vespa downstairs. Why don't we race around on it and try to get those guys together and then we can go get Patch?"

"Let's do it!" Arno yelled. He popped Mickey's board into the air and it shot across the room and smashed a framed Andy Warhol print of Mick Jagger that Ricardo

Pardo had given to his son for his thirteenth birthday.

"Sorry, dude," Arno said.

"Whatever," Mickey said. "My dad's being a dick lately anyway. Let's roll."

david gets back to where he was before

"Are you sure you didn't have sex with her?" Amanda Harrison Deutschmann asked. She had her arms folded over her chest and was leaning against the windowsill in David's bedroom, which didn't look a lot different than it did when David was thirteen—he still had the Nakamichi stereo he'd bought with his bar mitzvah money and old posters of Alan Iverson and Latrell Sprewell. Other than that the room was messy, with schoolbooks and sports clothes on the floor and a corner devoted to sneakers that Jonathan had said weren't cool.

"Yes," David said.

"Yes, what?"

Night had fallen, but the sky was still bright, as it always was with all the lights in Manhattan. Amanda was wearing impossibly tight low-cut jeans, black suede high heels, and a black silk turtleneck.

David was slowly putting on the new sneakers he'd gotten with Jonathan. It was nearly seven and David knew he had to go find his friends, but Amanda was having trouble believing that he'd done nothing with Kelli. This made sense to David. He was having trouble saying it.

"Yes, baby. I'm sure we didn't have sex."

"Since when did you start calling me 'baby'?"

"You don't like it?"

"No," Amanda said, "I guess I do. It's just . . . there's something different about you. And if it's not because you fooled around with that skeez from wherever, it's for some other reason. Tell me the truth, David, what'd you do with her?"

"We talked. That's all. Ask her yourself."

David sat back. He thought, *this is called lying.* Like what Arno and everybody else did. Maybe they'd fooled around. And maybe he'd fooled around with that other girl, too, for a second. But they were the first girls he'd ever, ever cheated on Amanda with, and now he was even with her, right? Assuming they really were getting back together. And he was feeling so cool that he wasn't even sure he wanted to. But after all, she'd called him.

"I'm so sorry for the way I treated you," Amanda said. He wanted her to say that again, but he knew better than to ask. "Really, David. There's something . . . it's like . . . um, I want you."

"Oh yeah?"

235

"David?" His mother opened his door and came in. Amanda glared at her.

"Oh, hello, Amanda."

"Hi."

"How are you?"

"I'm fine."

Then nobody spoke. David slowly took the pins out of his new Paul Smith button-down shirt. He held it up, but at the last minute he decided not to put it on.

"Well, your dad and I are going out," Mrs. Grobart said. "You understand, don't you? You won't feel that we're leaving you here alone, without guidance? Because we can stay in if you do feel that way."

"We'll be fine," Amanda said.

"Mmm," Mrs. Grobart said. "We're having dinner with the Fradys."

Nobody said anything. Hilary Grobart stood in the doorway, biting her lip.

"Have you two eaten anything?"

"We're okay," David and Amanda said, nearly in unison.

Mrs. Grobart closed the door behind her and Amanda and David looked at each other.

"We're alone now," Amanda said. She went over to David's stereo and put in a mix she'd been carrying around. It was mostly instrumental stuff and a bunch of

Radiohead and Rufus Wainright songs that were guaranteed to bring tears to just about anybody's eyes. The music got going and for a full minute, Amanda didn't turn around. David stared at her back and felt the prickly edge that he'd gained the night before soften. He wanted her.

"Amanda," he said.

She looked at him. Her eyes were glistening. She walked over to where he was sitting on his bed and sat down next to him.

"I love you," she said.

David took off his new shoes. They pushed the scratchy blanket off the bed and lay down. Later, after they'd dozed for a little while instead of really talking about anything, she said, "You need to go find your friends. I heard you're all going to look for Patch."

"I know. I'm going to get up in a second." It was nearly eight. His phone had rung a couple of times. They lay in his bed for a while longer, kissing. And he thought about all the crazy stuff that had happened the night before and all the crazy stuff that was going to happen as soon as he met up with his friends. He squeezed his eyes shut. He held her.

"You weren't nice to me," he said.

"I was afraid of being vulnerable with you."

"Why?"

"Because you're so unembarrassed to be in love. It's weird."

"I'm sorry," David said.

"No. I guess it's not that big of a problem."

And then they got dressed and slipped out of his apartment. David raced over to Mickey's place, and Amanda went to find Liza. She was becoming a different person, David thought. He felt so incredibly lucky that he hadn't lost her. Not to Arno, and not to all the stuff he'd done the night before.

a perfectly normal dinner with my family

"Aren't you going to be late?" I asked. I was sitting at the dinner table in my apartment and I was seriously itching to leave. But I couldn't. My mom was at the head of the table, sitting next to her nearly identical sister, Kelli's mom. And Kelli was next to me. It was nearly eight. My mom and Kelli's mom were going to see *La Boheme* at Lincoln Center. And Kelli and I had been gathered up for a family dinner delivered by a special chef from Tomoe Sushi. I actually sort of knew the chef, who was hanging around in the kitchen, playing with our knives. Mickey used to buy pot from him.

"Probably," my mom said. "But the first half hour is nothing special."

"Actually the whole first act is nothing terrific," her sister said. Both women laughed.

"And we've got Andy downstairs. He can get us there in ten minutes." The sisters were drinking huge goblets of red wine. Kelli and I were drinking wine, too, and we were seriously glaring at each other. Then my Blackberry went off. Arno: *Ten minutes*. I didn't know where everybody was but I did know that if I didn't get out of my house in less than that ten minutes my head would probably spin off my shoulders.

My mom and her sister were deep into their own conversation, which seemed to center around other people's divorces. They'd run into several of their friends at Canyon Ranch, and now they were picking them apart, one by one.

I watched Kelli. I kept shaking my head at her. She had rocked my little group awfully hard since she'd arrived. And I felt a little played by her. More than a little. Her phone rang and she checked the name, rolled her eyes, and let it go to voice mail. Now she had two phones and a pager, all given to her by different people who wanted to be able to reach her. At this rate, Kelli was going to have knapsack full of communication devices that she'd have to drag around so she could hear from all her suitors. It was nuts. And what was even more nuts was that her mom seemed to be pretending not to notice. Kelli was wearing a black velvet blazer and a ripped pink

T-shirt underneath that said *Lick Me.* Subtle.

"What are you doing tonight?" I asked. Her eyeliner was smudged and she looked deathly pale. I wasn't sure if the look was intentional.

"Nothing," she said.

"Yeah, right."

"There's a party in Chinatown," she said. "But it's a much older crowd. I probably won't see you there."

"Wow, in the four or five years you've been here you've really gotten to know the scene," I said.

"Shut up," Kelli said simply. "Some people were born to drive this town wild, and I'm one of them."

"You're crazy," I said.

"You're jealous."

"You're leaving tomorrow."

"We'll just see about that."

Kelli's other phone rang. This was a Treo handheld computer about the size of a deck of cards. It looked like it cost a thousand dollars and it probably had enough power to direct air traffic. She took the call.

"Yeah? . . . Mr. Chow's? No, I haven't eaten dinner, not at all. Send a car for me, can't you?" Kelli stood up and walked out of the room. Neither of our mothers looked up.

"Um," I said. I pushed my hair out of my eyes. "How was Canyon Ranch?"

"It was extremely relaxing," my mom said as she speared a piece of yellowtail so fresh it was practically shivering and slipped it into her mouth. "Four days there and I can hardly remember why I felt all the nerves that forced me to go there in the first place, you know?"

"That's so well put," my aunt said. "I'd been concerned about Kelli and college, but now I can see that's ridiculous. She'll go wherever she wants to go."

"You don't know the half of it," I muttered.

"I'm out," Kelli called. The door slammed before anyone could say anything.

"You know," my mom said to her sister, "originally I was concerned about you two staying here. I was afraid of being overrun, so I booked a room at the Tribeca Grand for the two of you, in case we got into a spat. But I feel like we're girls again and we've totally abandoned our responsibilities. Isn't it fun?"

"Next time, I'll take the room," I said. Both women giggled at me. They were eating off of everyone's plates and clearly having *the best time*. I doubted they'd even make it to the opera.

My Blackberry went off again. Arno: *Time to go.*

"See you," I said, and left them to their sisterliness.

arno apologizes for real

"Ow," Arno said. Slowly, he got to his feet.

Mickey had popped an inadvertent wheelie on the way down Greenwich Street and Arno had flown off the back and nearly been run over by a Hummer.

When Mickey looked back to see what had happened, he'd swung around too quickly and the weight of his cast had made him lose control of the Vespa. It slid under the middle of one of those extra-long accordion buses, and the back tire had gotten crunched. Both boys were wide-eyed now and a little shaken. Mickey waved his cast around in the air.

"How messed up is it?" Arno asked.

"I don't know. I'll find out tomorrow," Mickey said. He quickly grabbed the Vespa out of the street and leaned it up against the side of a building. A doorman came out and Arno knew him slightly, because he'd been a frequent visitor to a girl who lived there the year before.

"Could you watch this?" Arno said to the doorman, and flipped him fifty bucks before the doorman said no.

"I've got an idea," Arno said. He hailed a cab, and they got in. "We'll go to my parents' house and see if there's a car."

"Sounds good," Mickey said. They got in touch with David and Jonathan. A few blocks later, they were in front of Arno's house.

Several limousines idled out front. They were all waiting for people who were having dinner inside. Arno scanned the drivers.

"Hey, Ezra," he said suddenly to a youngish guy in jeans and a T-shirt who was leaning against a black Cadillac Escalade. "Is that the cheesy piece of shit you're driving the Currins around in these days?"

Ezra nodded and winked at Arno. He'd been playing a computer game on his handheld.

"It's a lender," Ezra said. "The electric car's in the shop."

Arno nodded. Out of the corner of his eye, he saw Jonathan come up in a cab. Then David loped around the corner, on foot. Finally, the four of them were together.

"You want to take us somewhere?" Arno asked.

"What's in it for me?"

"There's a black Vespa on Greenwich that's a little fried but it's yours if you can drive us for a few hours."

Ezra nodded, and the four boys hopped into the Cadillac. The inside smelled new and everybody rolled down their windows. They all took a deep breath and relaxed.

"First things first," Jonathan said. Arno nodded.

"David, I'm sorry," Arno said. "There's no excuse for what I did."

"I'm going to keep going out with Amanda," David said. "And this is the last time you do this, right?"

"I swear I'll never fool around with a girl you like again," Arno said. "Hey, I'm happy for you and Amanda. She was just . . . she was just getting with me because she was afraid of the intensity of the thing she has with you."

"Now the two of you shake hands and we're a group again," Mickey said. And they did. Arno held David's hand for an extra moment, and he looked him in the eye.

"I really am sorry," Arno said.

"Just don't do it again," David said.

"On to the next subject," Mickey said. He checked his watch. Nearly nine. Everyone nodded. "Let's go to Siberia first and get a cocktail."

"Where's your new shoes?" Jonathan said to David.

"Oh, I guess I forgot to put them on."

"And the shirt?"

David shrugged. Jonathan frowned. David was wearing the same outfit he always wore.

"He doesn't need to dress cool to be cool," Arno said suddenly. "Isn't that right, David?" David stared at him.

246

"Yeah," David said slowly. "I guess that's right."

"That outfit was important to me," Jonathan said.

"Dude!" Mickey said. "Do not say things like that."

"Yeah," Arno agreed. "We're all into clothes and all that crap, but the way you talk about what people are wearing, like it's *important*. I mean, stop before I puke all over the place."

"If you do puke, watch out for your four-hundred-dollar alligator Gucci loafers."

"Fine," Arno said. "But I don't think about it. Just like David doesn't think about how he's been wearing the same sweatshirt for three years."

"Yeah," David said. "Jonathan, after we find Patch we're going to go to work on your values."

"Oh, *shut up*," Jonathan said. But everyone else was laughing.

Arno felt relieved. David didn't hate him anymore. He was back, and his friends were into him. Nobody was going to hate each other forever.

"Drinks are on me," Arno said.

"Cool," Ezra said from the driver's seat. "I called some people already."

They arrived in front of Siberia. It was dark out and cars flew by on the West Side Highway.

"What happens if we don't find Patch?" Jonathan asked.

"We're going to find him," everyone else said. "We have to."

They all spilled out of the Escalade and of course Kelli was there, with Randall Oddy and a whole bunch of older people.

"Damn," Arno said.

"It doesn't matter," Jonathan said. "You're over her."

"Yeah," Arno said. But he knew that was only about 49 percent true. He closed his eyes and tried to remember the shower he'd taken with Mariela just a few hours before. Forget this, remember that. He said that to himself about a million times in one second, but then Kelli smiled at him.

"Hi," Kelli said. "I was just leaving. There's this party in Chinatown that's supposed to be absolutely incredible."

"We're going there, too," Mickey said. "Remember, this came up last night?"

Mickey had come out of nowhere. Arno was impressed. After falling off the Vespa, Mickey probably needed to go to the hospital again.

"In fact," Mickey said, "we're friends with one of the hosts."

Arno snapped his fingers and winked at his good bud, as if to say *thanks, man.*

"Whatever," Kelli said.

the object of our affection

My phone rang and I took the call.

"I hope you're looking for my brother," Flan said.

"We are. Where've you been?"

"That doesn't matter. But if he's not home by 10:00 A.M., we're all going to be in a lot of trouble."

"We'll find him. Why haven't I seen you?"

"Just get my brother," Flan said. And clicked off. I arched an eyebrow, but said nothing. I didn't want to hear more from anybody about how I should deal with Flan.

We spilled out onto the street in front of a steel door down at the bottom of the Bowery, at the foot of the Manhattan Bridge. The sidewalks smelled of fish and beer and people from outside the city who were finishing big dinners and slowly walking back to their cars. We looked up, beyond the restaurants, to the lofts that dotted the upper floors of the dark buildings.

"I can feel him," I said.

"He is near," Mickey said. He pulled out a rope and started to swing it up to a fire escape, but Arno grabbed him.

"This is somebody's house—we need to go through the door," Arno said.

Of course we didn't have the exact address, so we had to wait and watch and see if we could follow anyone in. Sure enough, a couple of those teenage models who are freakishly thin and good-looking but have absolutely nothing to say wandered down the street and rang a buzzer on a door about ten feet from where we stood.

"You guys going to Graca's?" one of them asked. She had on thick black eyeliner and she was wearing a blouse with a tadpole silk-screened on it.

"Yeah," Mickey said quickly. We rode up with them in a rickety old elevator, the six of us holding a collective breath.

"What if he's not here?" I whispered. Mickey, David, and Arno shook their heads, like don't even think that.

"He'll be there," the other model said, even though there was no way she could know who we were talking about. "*Everybody* goes to Graca's."

We got out at the top floor and wandered into a loft that was eerily quiet. At one end, far down from where we were, under a skylight that bathed everyone in dark blue, there was a dinner party going on. Music played—some Eurotrash pop that I didn't recognize—and slowly we made our way toward the group. Behind us, I could hear more people coming up the stairs.

"Wow," David said.

"It's cool," I whispered. "They're in that transition moment, between when a party is all about dinner and then it turns into a blowout, you know?"

"Dude, could you please not overanalyze," Mickey said.

The table was long and wide, with at least twenty people sitting at it. At the far end, a woman was seated next to an empty chair. The models were saying hello to the woman, who had to be around twenty-one. Graca, they called her. She was Spanish or Brazilian or something, and totally stunning, with long black hair and big black eyes set wide apart. The four of us stopped and stood there, because we didn't know a

251

person in the place.

"This is awkward," I said.

"It really is," David said.

Then a door opened even farther back in the loft, and we saw Patch come out. He came over and kissed Graca, and he was weirdly beaming as he took his seat. He hadn't seen us.

"Is there more Rioja?" he asked. Graca smiled and rumpled Patch's hair. The music switched to the soundtrack from *Y Tu Mama Tambien*.

Then Patch looked up. We'd just been staring at him. It was hard to deal with the idea that he was missing when he was sitting in the middle of some dinner party.

"Hey . . . ," he said, and wandered over to us. "It's you guys." He was wearing the same khakis he had on when we'd last seen him, and a black T-shirt that didn't fit him right and clearly belonged to a girl. No shoes. His hair was rumpled. He came up and hugged me.

"Where the hell have you been?" I asked.

"What?" Patch asked. "Oh, I've been here." He smiled at the four of us and we surrounded him in a circle. "It was like, last week sometime, I forget when, I was skateboarding in Union Square and I fell, and this girl picked me up and it was

Graca." He glanced over his shoulder, and she waved. "And she took me home, and we've been here ever since. She makes leather pants for rock stars. Isn't that cool?"

"We've been worried about you."

"Really?" Patch said. "That's cool."

I looked around and just shook my head. A mirror propped by the door had claimed Arno's attention, and Mickey, who'd found Patch's skateboard, started to ride around the empty front of the loft. David was hanging back, probably uncomfortable among all the beautiful Brazilians.

"So you're good," I said.

"Uh, better than that, dude. But you're right, I should check in with my sisters, at least."

"They've been covering for you with your parents," I said.

"Yeah, they're good that way."

And again, I just shook my head. No wonder some insanely hot Brazilian leather pants designer had taken Patch home. I mean, he was the most laid-back, good-looking kid in New York.

Patch and I went over to the table and he introduced me around. He handed me a glass of Rioja.

"You'll love this," he said.

I took a sip, and it was good.

"But you need to go home soon," I said. "At least check in for brunch tomorrow."

"I guess you're right," Patch said. A serious expression passed over his face, but then it disappeared.

"How's Flan?"

"Good," I said, and left it at that. I wondered where she was, and why she wouldn't tell me. Some people started to dance. Graca drifted up from the table and began to dance in a circle with a few other women. She smiled over at us.

"Isn't she amazing?" Patch said. "We kept meaning to do stuff. Like she should work and I should go to school, and call people, and all that, but we kept forgetting."

Patch threw his arm around me, and we stood there, drinking wine and just sort of digging on the scene. I felt totally calm and then I realized that I hadn't felt that way in a while, not since my cousin Kelli had come to town.

Then there was a noise at the door, someone knocking really loud and not realizing that the door was unlatched, so it suddenly flew open and banged against the wall with an ugly crunching sound. Randall Oddy came in with Kelli and five guys, who were all smiling and totally focused on

Kelli. She scoped the scene and saw that she knew only me and my people, so she smiled wide, like we hadn't been fighting for days and now she was happy to run into me.

"Jonathan!" Kelli yelled as she came running over to us.

"That's my cousin," I said to Patch.

"She's . . . loud," Patch said. I smiled. Patch wasn't into loudness.

"Hey, who's this?" Kelli asked. As usual, a couple of guys were trailing her. She grinned at Patch and her grin said, *should I be sampling you?*

"Oh no you don't," I said. "You already messed up two of my friends. I don't even want you talking to this one."

"Hey," Kelli said. "I'm harmless."

"No you're not."

"I'm Patch," Patch said. And he shook hands with Kelli. He smiled at her. And Kelli smiled back.

"And I'm Graca," Graca said. Her voice was like hot butter and she rolled her *r*s. She'd stopped dancing and walked over to us. Arno and David and Mickey had all made their way to us, too, and now we all stood there, staring at her.

She was so beautiful. Patch kissed her.

"Do you all want some wine?" Graca asked.

"Yes," we said. I emptied my glass and she went toward where the kitchen must have been.

"I'm in love," Patch said. We all nodded at him. We could see why.

"Excuse me," Kelli said. "I think someone's calling my name." But nobody paid attention to her, and so she walked away.

"You need to remember to go home," Mickey said to Patch.

"Not till tomorrow morning."

"But definitely then," Arno said. "We'll get you there. It's good to see you, man, we really missed you."

"But I thought you forgot about me."

"Well, yeah," I said. "We did for a while. But I'm still really happy to see you now."

"Okay," Patch said. He smiled the easy smile that had been keeping him out of trouble since he'd been born.

a little more from the social glue

Toward four in the morning, Graca ran out of wine and I was having trouble keeping everything in focus. Patch hadn't disappeared again, which was a good thing. He was dancing with Graca. And Kelli was dancing with Randall Oddy and Arno was sort of between the two couples, dancing with the model with the tadpole on her shirt.

David came over to where I was sitting at the dinner table. I'd been picking at a plate of olives, and penciling a drawing of Flan on a napkin.

"I'm tired," David said. "I called my mom and said I was staying at your house. I hope that's not a problem."

"Nope, so long as she knows that tonight my house is a suite at the Tribeca Grand."

"She doesn't know that," David said. "Did your mom sell your apartment?"

"I'm kidding," I said. "But there is a room in

my mom's name at the Grand. It's probably a suite. We can all crash there."

"I guess that's cool," David agreed.

I saw Ezra the driver dance by.

He said, "Hey, you know Kelli? She's cool."

And I just shook my head and pretended not to hear him. Arno's model was clearly sick for him, and I mean sick. She hung on him like they were lost at sea and he was a life preserver. But he was still looking around for Kelli.

"Jonathan?"

I turned around and it was Fernanda, from Barneys. That girl, she glowed.

I said, "Let's dance."

She was carrying a highball glass that she must have brought from another party and she was trailed by five or six people who were so well dressed they simply had to be her friends from work.

"You know Graca?" she asked.

"I know Patch," I said. She smiled, as if that made everything okay, and we began a slow dance.

"Hi, Fernanda," someone said. Kelli.

"Dammit, Kelli!" I yelled. "Your knowing everybody ruins everything for everyone else!"

"Whoa," Fernanda said. She took a step back.

"Why are you so threatened by it?" Kelli asked.

"Because nobody learns New York in a week," I said. Well, maybe I spluttered. David, who'd been furiously making out with Amanda, who'd showed up with Liza and Jane, looked up.

"It's destiny," Kelli said simply.

"Bullshit," I said. "You turned all my friends against each other and made me lose sight of Patch!"

I immediately whipped around. Patch was nowhere in sight.

"You did it again!" I yelled.

"You're ridiculous," Kelli said. She turned to Fernanda. "How's Barnard?" she asked.

And Fernanda frowned at me.

"Good. Do you have any additional questions, or did you feel like the tour I gave you was pretty comprehensive?"

"Oh," I said. I'd been pretty loud. People were looking. Where *was* Patch?

Fernanda smiled gently. She said, "You two do something together?"

"We're cousins," I said.

"Kissing cousins?"

"Hardly," I said.

I took Fernanda's hand and drew her toward me. She smelled faintly of Barneys. Or maybe what I loved about Barneys was the smell of her? Who cared? She was near me. I kissed her. Unfortunately, it lasted only about a second, till I felt voices calling my name.

"Did you lose Patch?" Mickey yelled. He was on the other side of the room, arguing with a bunch of Randall Oddy's friends. He could be pretty smart when he wanted to be.

"Did you?" Arno yelled. He was dancing with that model he'd picked up, Elizabetta.

"It's cool," David said. "He went home to show Flan he's okay. I saw him get in a cab."

"You sure?" I asked.

"Call Flan."

"No, not right now."

Fernanda was starting to walk away from me, and I caught up with her.

"You're not seeing me at my best," I said.

"I hope not," she said.

"It's been a stressful week," I said. "I had one of my best friends disappear, and my other friends all had some difficulties and it was really, really hard to keep track of everything. But if I could just see you some other time . . ."

"What?"

"You're amazing," I said.

"You know where to find me."

"In shoes," I said. And yeah, I sounded dreamy. She slipped away, and I let her go.

Then the weird thing happened when you're at the party for longer than you're supposed to be, and everything dissolves and it's just a room full of people you don't know very well, who all look kind of sweaty, and you need to run around and gather up your friends as quickly as possible, otherwise you'll end up in a cab alone. And nobody wants that. So I started whispering around about the suite at the Tribeca Grand.

Kelli heard me and said, "That's my suite." I couldn't totally disagree with her, since if she wanted to stay there, that was cool with me. I wanted her close right up to the moment when she walked onto the tarmac and onto United flight number Make-Things-Normal-Again.

Because the hotel was so close, the four of us and Kelli walked over and checked in. David fell asleep on a big white sharkskin chair. Kelli shared the sofa with Arno, and I listened to them talking about how strongly he felt and she sounded like she was being kind of patient with him about it. I took the big bed with Mickey, who was passed out before he had his shoes off. Outside, I could see the sun start to rise. I closed my eyes. But Mickey smelled so strongly of alcohol that I had to stuff tissues up my nose.

"Hey, Jonathan."

"What?" I asked. It was Kelli. She gotten up from the other room and now she was standing over me.

"I know I was a little more than you'd bargained for but I guess . . . I want to thank you."

"What for, idiot?" I said. But I sort of smiled up at her. Mickey smelled so bad. I wondered when he ever changed his jumpsuit.

"Thanks for letting me come out with you."

"Well," I said.

Kelli sat down at the edge of the bed. Her hair was sticking up in places and her new Helmut Lang pants were stiff, too. But her arms were kind of thin and innocent. She was like that—about the most innocent thing about her were her forearms.

"Sorry if I screwed up your life and made you lose track of your friend."

"I guess it's not really your fault," I said.

"Except for the part where you nearly totally destroyed all my friends' relationships."

"Kelli?" Arno said.

Kelli smiled at me. "He said he'd cry unless I held him tight."

"You're the first girl who ever said no to him."

"Shut up," Arno said.

"I say no to everybody," Kelli said.

"Except me," David said, and smiled in his sleep.

Kelli stood up then, and through the curtains, the city had begun to glow behind her. Then, just as I was falling off for a much-needed few hours of sleep, I heard Kelli go back over and lie down next to Arno.

"You're a pain in the ass," Arno said.

"You're worse, rich boy," Kelli said.

And then they went on and began arguing in that way that inevitably means you're going to fool around, and pretty seriously, too, if nobody stops you, which I certainly wasn't going to, because I was asleep by then, and the bed was comfortable. And if two people who were sort of made for each other but didn't really like each other at all were going to get into something serious, who was I to stop them?

sunday brings us near to our end

the flood family actually sits down together

The croissants were golden and flaky, and their hot pastry smell washed over everything. At the table in the downstairs dining room, just off the kitchen, sat five Floods: Frederick and his wife, Fiona, Flan, February, and Patch, who had his eyes closed and was still listening to music from the night before.

"How was St. Lucia?" Flan said to her mom. Flan was wearing her riding clothes, including her brown velvet helmet with the chin strap done up. They'd asked her repeatedly to take it off, but she said she liked to be prepared, because she planned to go riding with a special someone. She wouldn't say who that was.

"What?" Fiona Flood asked.

"Weren't you there?"

Fiona shot a look at her husband. Frederick was slathering a croissant with butter.

"Have some croissant with your butter?" Fiona asked, and frowned. "I was there, yes. For a few days, for a much-needed rest from your father."

"Doesn't anyone want to hear about how my job is going?" February asked. She'd come in from her night two hours before, at eight in the morning, but the elder Floods had been out in the garden, discussing what to do with the rosebushes. Retrench or pare back?

"What about it?" Frederick said.

"It sucks," February said.

"This orange juice is fantastic," Patch said. It was all he could think of to say. It wasn't that he didn't like his family, he just didn't get them. Even his little sister Flan was slowly getting lost on him. She made a pouty face all the time, and it was confusing that she'd gotten so good-looking and was only in eighth grade.

He sipped the juice, which was fresh. The scrambled eggs had bits of salmon and chive flecked through them. Patch ate quietly, with his head down.

"We may be headed back up to Greenwich, mid-week," Frederick said.

Flan stared down at her plate and adjusted her helmet. She helped herself to more eggs. Of course February was only drinking coffee, black.

"How's Zed doing?" Fiona asked.

But nobody said anything, because nobody really knew.

"This is the best coffee," Patch said as he sipped at it. He didn't like to drink a lot of coffee, because he didn't like to be that awake, but he couldn't think of what else to say. During the silence that followed, the entire family began to stare at him. He looked at his plate.

"What?" Patch said. He smiled at them, his crinkly smile that made everybody feel good and got them to leave him alone at the same time.

"How's Mickey?" his mother asked. "I think we're seeing the Pardos tomorrow night or the next for the symphony. Anything special we should know about?"

"Yes, how are your friends?" Frederick asked. Then he seemed to remember something, and got up and went back to the kitchen.

"Well," Patch said. "Um. I think they had a tough week."

"Why?"

"Um." Patch looked at the hem of his khakis, at the freckles on his arm. He smiled. He thought, *Graca*. He wanted to see her, and desire washed over him. He'd told her he'd see her later, but what had he meant? He needed to see her now. He wondered how to do it.

"Mickey broke his arm," Flan said.

"He slipped on some stairs at school," February said. Both his sisters were staring at Patch, slight grins on their faces.

"What about Zed?" Frederick said on his way back

into the room.

"Dad," Flan said, "Zed is at Vassar."

"We can still talk about him, can't we?" Frederick asked. And suddenly all of the Floods looked confused. *How was Zed doing?*

"Let's call," Fiona said. "Who has his number?"

Just then the family dog, Fido, came running in. She'd been up in Greenwich. She was a big dog, a retriever mixed with a St. Bernard—floppy and excited. Patch dropped onto the floor to play with her while the family discussed calling their eldest son.

"Has anyone walked Fido?" Patch asked.

Nobody responded. Flan was hitting herself on the helmet with her riding crop. February was leaned so far back in her chair that it looked as if she were about to pass out. From his vantage point on the floor, Patch could see her fingering a cigarette. Frederick rubbed the sleeve of his orange cashmere sweater against his clean-shaven cheek.

"Perhaps we ought to drive up to Boston and see him?" Frederick said.

"Dad!" the two girls said.

"I know, I know, Vassar's in Washington," Frederick said. The family laughed, if not heartily.

"Let's go, girl," Patch said. He slipped a white leather leash onto Fido's collar. The dog licked Patch's ears. On the way out, Patch grabbed a jacket off the coat tree by the front door. It happened to be his father's four-thousand-dollar Paul Stuart shearling coat, but Patch didn't notice. He only thought, this feels soft.

Outside, the day was beautiful and cool. Patch began to walk Fido downtown. He didn't know where he was going. Then he did. *Graca.*

arno's dreamgirl goes home

"Wake up," Jonathan said. Arno opened one eye and looked straight up into Jonathan's frowning face.

Arno was in bed with Kelli, legs intertwined under a sheet. Kelli instantly stood up and went to the bathroom. Four boys' heads swiveled and watched her go as she dragged the sheet off a very naked Arno.

"Put your shorts on, hotstuff," Jonathan said. "We've got a plane to catch."

"You go," Arno said, and fell back against the pillows. On the couch, Mickey began to stir. Somehow, during the night, everyone had switched places. David was over by the windows, calmly explaining to his mother why she hadn't been able to reach him at Jonathan's house.

"There's no bigger explanation, Mom," David said. "I'd tell you if there was, I swear. No, not with Jonathan. I promise. I slept in a chair."

"Dude," Mickey sputtered as he sat up, "David's mom thinks you want to sleep with David."

Jonathan didn't seem to notice. He said, "I called Ezra. He's psyched about the Vespa, we're going to eat at Bubby's, and then he'll help us get my cousin out of town."

"What are you talking about?" Arno said, and quickly sat up and looked around. The room was a mess. There were clothes and glasses everywhere.

"She's leaving, that's what I'm talking about."

Arno stood up and went into the bathroom, where Kelli was. She looked up at him. She was on her phone. He stood in front of her.

"Yes, I promise to see you at practice tomorrow," Kelli said.

She smiled at Arno and kissed his cheek. Arno tried to smile, but he was so confused that his face sort of bent, and he looked as if someone had just slapped him. Kelli ended the call.

"Take a shower with me," she said.

"Do I have to wait in line?" Arno asked. They glared at each other like a couple who had been going out for all of freshman and sophomore and into junior year.

"We're ready when you two are," Jonathan yelled through the door. "Brunch is on me."

"Don't go," Arno said to Kelli.

"Oh, don't start," Kelli said.

Everyone got themselves together and they walked

the few blocks over to Bubby's. They got a table for five against the back wall, where it was cool and bright and the sun shone through special skylights that filtered out the UV rays. Jonathan ordered a pitcher of mimosas.

"This is nice," Kelli said. Then she immediately stood up and went over to a table populated by several male actors and introduced herself.

"There's something about her, I'd do anything for her," Arno said as he watched her. From a dozen feet away, they could hear her saying, "You're going to direct? How cool—I'm thinking of getting into acting."

"Ezra's coming here in half an hour," David said. "We slam down some eggs Benedict and the mimosas and then we're out of here."

"I told my mom to pack Kelli's bags," Jonathan said. "And send them with her mom. Look, Arno, it's nice that you hooked up with her, but we have absolutely got to get this girl out of town."

While they watched, several men at the other table made room for Kelli and she settled in between them. She immediately starting drinking one guy's Bloody Mary through a straw.

"I don't know if we should wait for our food," David said.

"Why?" Arno asked.

Just then a waitress arrived. She was short and her

hair was piled high on her head.

"Hey, Chloe," Arno said.

The waitress smiled.

"I'm sorry I haven't called you," Arno said. "If you weren't on shift, when I got my French toast we could do stuff to each other with the maple syrup."

"If you really want to know how good that'd feel," she said, "ask that one."

She gestured at David, who'd been looking at his knees. When it grew quiet, David looked up.

"Oh, hey," David said. "We met on Friday night."

The other guys at the table stared at David.

"I'm just glad you're back with Amanda," Arno said, once the waitress had left. "I sure as hell wouldn't want to compete for girls with you."

"Thanks," David said. "Hey, look who it is. How are you, man?"

The four boys turned around and Flan Flood was standing at their table. She was wearing her riding out-fit and there was somebody next to her. Adam Rickenbacher.

"I'm good," Adam said, and smiled.

"No," Jonathan said. He reached for his glass but missed it. And then he was just staring up at Flan and Adam. They were holding hands.

"Ouch," Arno said.

"We're looking for Patch," Flan said to everyone at the table but Jonathan, who she cut with her eyes in a way that would serve her well in high school. "He took Fido for a walk this morning and didn't come back. Have you guys seen him?"

"I lose sight of Patch for one second," Jonathan said to Flan, "and you're standing there with another guy."

"I hope there isn't a problem," Adam said.

"No, it's cool," Mickey said. "Why don't you two scoot along. We know where Patch is."

Jonathan made a gurgling sound in his throat. Adam and Flan walked out of the restaurant. But then Flan came running back and bent down over Jonathan, who was looking shocked and still hadn't said anything.

"I waited and waited, but you wouldn't make a move," she said. And then she ran out again.

None of the other guys said anything. Jonathan really did look sick, like he'd messed up a good thing.

"That's for the best," Arno said. "Anyway, it's nearly eleven."

Outside, Ezra pulled up in the Escalade.

Arno looked over at the other table. Kelli was doing something that looked like acting for the would-be director. He was taking her picture with a digital camera and she was roaring like a big cat. She pushed aside the bread basket and some plates of eggs and climbed up on the table.

"Let's go," Mickey said.

"But we haven't even eaten," Arno said. His jaw had gone slack and he was staring at Kelli.

"RRRrr," Kelli growled from the other table.

"Let's go before someone gets really hurt," Jonathan said. He stood up and slowly his guys followed his example. They went over to the actors' table and picked up Kelli, who was now lying down and purring for the camera.

"Sorry, boys," Arno said. "If I can't have her, only a quarterback in St. Louis can."

Arno and David and Mickey and Jonathan each took one of Kelli's limbs and carried her out of the restaurant. Though they did get some stares, Kelli wasn't recognizably famous, so everyone assumed she was drunk or something.

"She just got blown away by the city and she wouldn't stop," Jonathan said, in explanation to Ezra, who held the door to the Escalade open as they put Kelli inside.

"Shut up," Kelli said. "I'm coming back here and you can't stop me."

"Be nice to Jonathan," Arno said. "He just got completely and unexpectedly played."

"To LaGuardia Airport," Jonathan said. "And hurry."

fernanda, or flan?

"It wasn't any one thing about Kelli," I said to Fernanda.

"I don't get it," Fernanda said. "What was the problem?"

"She was like, desperate for attention."

"Aren't we all?"

"Yeah, but we don't double-cross everyone we meet to get it."

We walked quietly for a moment. We were on Fifth Avenue and Sixteenth Street, in front of the Paul Smith men's store. Out of habit, I stopped and stared in the window. I'm not normally partial to Paul Smith, because the clothes tend toward the frilly, but I kept looking, just to see if they'd changed or anything. There was a pair of reddish velvet loafers that very, very few men could have pulled off. They did have a nice cut to them, though, very long and angular. Not a JM Weston or a Crockett and Jones shoe cut, not that nice, but nice. And when I looked down—and I must've been staring at those shoes for a full minute—I was holding Fernanda's hand.

"Let's walk over to Otto and get some pizza and ice cream," I said suddenly.

"You don't want to go in here and try stuff on?"

"No, I don't think so."

Fernanda smiled at me. We kept walking on Fifth. It was nearly seven on Tuesday evening and the street was quiet and kind of cool, in a really good end-of-October way.

"The thing is," I said, "I've got these friends I have to take care of, and when I do a lousy job and forget one of them, they disappear."

"You know that's crazy, right?" Fernanda said.

"Yeah, it is," I said. "But I lost track of Patch again and now no one knows where he is."

"What do you mean? He's living with Graca. His parents are annoyed, but he's going to school and just sort of hanging with her. The whole family was driving him crazy. All those F names. It was too much. We all know that."

"Sure, we know that. But . . ."

I looked over at Fernanda. Since we'd been basically inseparable for the last couple of days, there was definitely a way to think of her as my girlfriend, if I wanted to be comfortable with that, which I'm pretty sure I did want.

And further, I was happy that Flan had hooked up with that Rickenbacher kid, whom I still didn't much like. I mean, good for her. And good for Liza for also being totally over me.

But about Flan . . . she wouldn't speak to me. Wouldn't even return my calls. And I didn't necessarily think that was a bad thing. Not that I thought we should ever go out or anything. I didn't. But it was nice to know she wasn't treating me like a big brother. And I figured I'd call her again, just to see if she wanted to hang out sometime or something. Because, I figured, we still should be able to be friends. And I missed her.

"Are you thinking of that kid, Flan?"

"No," I said quickly.

We kept walking, down toward Otto. A guy and a girl on a bright red Vespa went hurtling by. They were laughing and weaving, and the girl had a long red scarf that made a whistling noise in the wind. It was Mickey and Philippa. They were still in love.

"Right now, I don't want to keep track of anybody but you," I said to Fernanda. I held up her hand and kissed it.

Don't miss the next instalment of
The Insiders . . .

Rumors are spreading fast about Jonathan
and his friends.

Who will hook up?

Who will get dumped?

And what happens when the guys betray
each other?

While you wait for the next book, check
out what's new with the Insiders at
www.insidersbook.com.